Icebound

CORINNA ROGERS

HarperImpulse an imprint of
HarperCollins*Publishers* Ltd
77–85 Fulham Palace Road
Hammersmith, London W6 8JB

www.harpercollins.co.uk

A Paperback Original 2014

First published in Great Britain in ebook format by HarperImpulse 2014

A catalogue record for this book is
available from the British Library

ISBN: 978-0-00-811560-9

Automatically produced by Atomik ePublisher from Easypress

CORINNA ROGERS

I've always wanted to tell stories for a living and I can't stand the idea that the only great story to be told in romance is will-they-or-won't-they – especially when there's a whole other world to explore through the looking glass once they do finally get together! Exploring the unseen side of relationships, exploring what makes characters special when they're in awful situations, exploring how a book can grab you and refuse to let you go – those are the passions that drive my storytelling. I love world-building, I love language, and I love hearing people speak about something that makes them truly passionate. I love books that you can fall into like comfortable furniture, and trust them to take you for a ride through haunted woods. I want people to feel challenged and delighted rather than simply amused and distracted. I believe in the power of entertainment, and I hope to share some of the stories and characters that live in my mind.

Having studied, lived and taught in California, New York, London and Japan, I now live in North Carolina with the love of my life and too many cats. If you would like to find out more about me and my books, you can follow me on Twitter @Corinna_Rogers.

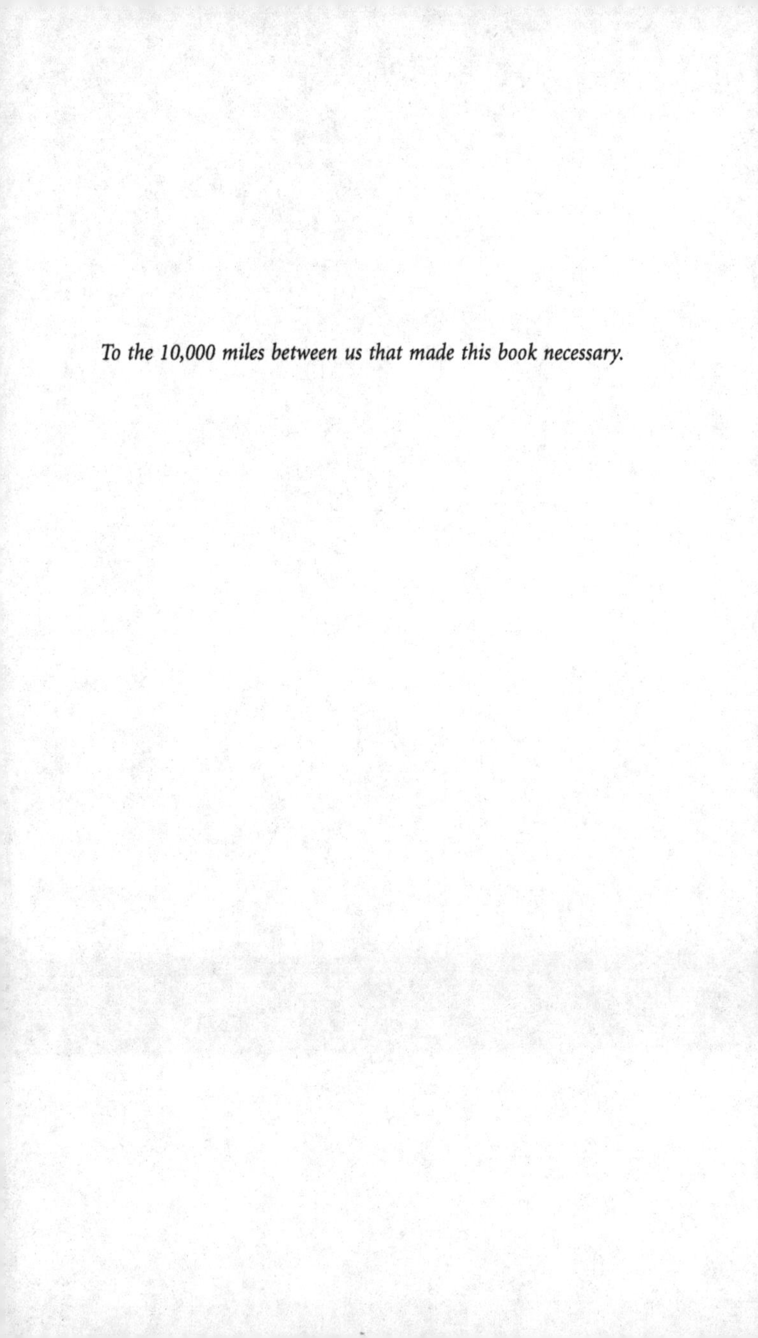

To the 10,000 miles between us that made this book necessary.

Chapter One

Ice creeps up the window, spider-webbing out to cover the glass pane completely. Shane watches it, amused, because it's better than watching the ceiling, waiting for the knock on his door. The TV is on, some shitty program about parenthood and people who shouldn't be allowed within five hundred yards of it, and for a second it's a struggle to remember why he shouldn't just throw it out the window.

The knock is tentative at first, soft, and that pisses him off. "Get in here."

The man who enters is tall, just over six feet, and broadly muscled, enough that he'd be able to toss the TV out the window with one hand and little effort. He's got an open, honest face, smooth and darker-skinned than Shane, whether from his mother's Portuguese heritage or his own tendency to forget about sunscreen whenever he leaves the house. His hair falls in dark-brown waves to the top of his back, accenting the strength in his chin, his straight nose, his rough, capable hands. There's a hint of beauty about him, for all that he looks like he could be hit by a truck and apologize for denting the fender, accenting his cheekbones, his eyelashes, the little dip below his collarbone that Shane knows so well.

It doesn't matter how many times the man comes here. It never stops making Shane's heart ache. "I like those jeans. They make your ass look fantastic."

"I was hoping you'd like them."

That voice – god. It sends ripples up his spine, and Shane lets his legs spread a bit, leaning back against the headboard. He almost slips up, almost says, I miss you, but that's too much. "Want your mouth," he says instead, and the other man nods, shutting the door behind him as he kneels on the bed between Shane's legs, hands sliding up his thighs.

Want to kiss you. It hurts, how much Shane wants to kiss him, but that's not part of the rules. Instead, he flicks open his own jeans one-handed, pulling himself out, already hard. "For such a big guy, you've got such a pretty mouth," he croons, twisting a hand in the man's hair. "Put it to good use. Don't flinch, you've been wanting this all day, haven't you?"

The man licks his lips, swallows hard, but nods. "Yeah. All day. Can I?"

Shane's hips twitch up at that question. It's so genuine, so wanting, for all that he knows it isn't. "Go on. See if you can take it all this time."

No matter how many times they've done this, it always feels like fucking heaven, the first swipe of that hot wet tongue over his cock. "Fuck, Drake. Such a good cocksucker. Good boy."

The praise spurs the man on, sliding his lips over the head of Shane's cock, moaning softly as he stretches his lips wide to take it all, inch by thick, hard inch.

It's the little details that make this so good. It's the drag of his tongue over the head of his cock, sure, but it's also the way Drake's eyelashes flutter, the way his hands splay out on Shane's thighs, the little noises he makes when Shane bucks up into the soft wet heat, making him gag.

"Go on, baby, *take* it. That's what you're here for, right? You didn't come here just to see my pretty face."

He loves the way it looks, his pale, flushed cock sliding into Drake's mouth, seeing the contrast of his skin against the tanned fingers of Drake's hands as they come up to try to steady himself, try to hold Shane down, but Shane's having none of it. He tightens his fingers in Drake's hair, and unless the other man wants a fight he has little choice but to swallow everything he's being given, the whole length of Shane down his throat.

He shouldn't love the tears in his eyes so much.

Shane guides him up and down, arm tense and strong on Drake's head, eventually just holding him in place while he fucks up into his mouth, relishing the choked wet sounds he forces from the other man's throat. It feels good, damned good to be using him like this, watching Drake gag on his cock without pulling away; if anything trying to take more of him in his mouth.

"Swallow for me," Shane breathes, and Drake just has time to nod once, quickly, before Shane fills his mouth, spilling over his tongue and watching eagerly as Drake's throat bobs, doing as he's told.

"Good boy," Shane murmurs, stroking the familiar brown hair, down the side of those smooth cheeks, suddenly finding it difficult not to let tears prick his own eyes. "God, baby, so good."

"I can stay. If you want me to."

The cold creeps back in. The window is entirely frosted over now, brittle enough that one hard blow would shatter the whole thing. "Stop it. You wouldn't say that."

Drake scowls at him, pushing off the bed, straightening his clothes. "Wouldn't be in your bed either, so maybe you should just get that stick out of your ass, boss."

"Take it off."

The man rolls his eyes, ripples, and instead of the familiar hard planes of Drake's body, a lithe young black man stands in Shane's room, hip insolently cocked. "You want anything else? I've got a hunt tonight."

"Give me his shirt back. I know it's his, it smells like him."

Slowly, Roy strips off the shirt, leaving him in just a pair of jeans that had been tight on Drake, now hanging baggy off his slender form. "You should check this one out, boss. Big prize."

"Not interested." Shane grabs the proffered item of clothing, not bothering to hide the way he buries his nose in it. Forest earth, clean cotton, the musk of a healthy human male all mix on the fabric, more familiar than the place he's in now. He'll probably have to punish Roy later for stealing from Drake—all his men know Drake is off-limits—but for now, he's glad.

"Soul-Thief. Eighty points on the rankings."

"Enjoy them."

"If I get it, I'm gonna be your boss before the week's out."

"Have fun. Leave me alone."

Roy shrugs, picking his way barefoot to the door, holding the baggy jeans up by one beltloop. He pauses with his hand on the doorknob. "Oh, and the King says to let you know that whoever bags the thing gets something back. Something of theirs."

The window cracks.

"What?"

"You heard me. You get it back if you bag the Soul-Thief."

A tremor of hungry need shoots through Shane, piercing the ice somehow, and he growls, "Get out."

The door slamming is too much for the frame, and the glass shatters. Cold wind blows in, fierce and shocking, but it does little to affect Shane. He doesn't even bother to do up his pants, staring instead at the closed door, hearing the words reverberating through his skull.

You get it back.

Those might be the words, but the meaning…

Oh, the meaning is a bit different.

You get him back.

Shane flicks on the TV and with a surge of power it changes from a teenage girl crying about her boyfriend not wanting to be a father to the inside of a martial arts studio. A dozen kids slowly punch and kick their way through beginner karate, calling out phrases in a language they don't speak as their pudgy little bodies struggle not to topple over.

The instructor, obviously, doesn't see it that way. "Good! Nice improvement. Keep your leg up, Jenny. Remember, keep that power in your core! Nice flexibility, wow, Jason, you've been practicing!"

Shane vaguely remembers watching Drake and not feeling pain. Now, pain is all he really feels.

His hair is short, which is always a startling reminder of how much time has passed, along with the short-cropped beard on his face, and the slight lines around his eyes, across his forehead. That's right, he's different now. It doesn't matter that it's only been a week since the last time he saw Drake in person. In Shane's mind, Drake always looks like he did back then, when everything was *good*.

The image zooms in on Drake's face, heartbreakingly familiar, and his eyes flicker suddenly, looking at the spell Shane's using in place of a camera. Very quietly, out of the corner of his mouth, he mutters, "Stop it. I can feel you watching me."

Shane doesn't stop. He doesn't bother to respond, by whispering into his ear or sending a chill breeze to hit him in the face. His continued presence is enough of a message.

It's not like he *can* stop anyway. All right, he probably could, but he has no desire to. It doesn't matter if Drake is angry with him, after all. He's always angry.

You get it back.

The hunts have been boring lately. It's always difficult to remind himself why he should bother climbing up the rankings when he's already at the top, has been for five years, and nothing's even a challenge anymore. But eighty points…

That's got to be challenging, at least a bit. Fae creatures are only fifteen, and they're the only big game the city sees on a semi-regular basis. It's been nearly a decade since there's been a bill posted for something over twenty, and Shane knows damned well that *that* hundred-point creature has never been caught.

Well, not in the traditional sense, with his head in a bag.

For a minute, Shane contemplates ignoring even this chance,

just flopping onto his bed and letting the chill wind lull him to sleep, maybe not even getting up. It's better than false hope. It's better than being stupid enough to believe that something could change for the better after all this time.

On the TV, Drake turns to give some fat kid some praise, and his smile is the most genuine thing Shane's ever seen. That spark of pain in his chest flares, and he chokes with how much it hurts.

"Fuck it," he mutters, grabbing a coat he doesn't need and a pistol he doesn't need and a sword he does. "Gotta be better than staying here."

Then again, anything would be.

Chapter Two

Finally, the sense of Shane's presence around his face vanishes. Drake Young breathes a sigh of not-quite-relief, turning his full attention back to the kids. "You're a little weak on your left side," he says with a poke to the child in question, illustrating the blind spot. "Make sure to keep your guard up."

They've all got such adoration in their eyes. Maybe he craves that a little too much, he admits to himself. It's nice to be liked. "All right. That's enough for the day. Practice the warm-up drill tomorrow, and I'll see you Thursday night."

They bow, uneven and exhausted, but with grins on their faces. A couple of them run up after class for a high-five, which he readily obliges. He checks his watch, but there's time, barely. He hops in the shower for a few minutes, always feeling that prickle of hesitation like he does every time he strips off, never sure if Shane's going to be watching.

What the hell, let him. Not like it's anything he hasn't seen before.

It isn't Shane, but his downstairs neighbor Deborah waiting for him when he gets to the door, a smile hovering uncertainly on her face. "Oh, good. I wasn't sure you'd still be here."

"Still here. Leaving now."

"Mind if I catch a ride home?"

He does, but nods anyway, mentally forgoing his plan to get groceries on the way home. "No problem. If you want, I'll go warm up the car."

"I don't mind a little cold." Deborah looks at him with naked hope in her eyes, trotting after his long legs into the cold night air. "I thought you only had classes until six."

"Most days. Monday nights I teach self-defense, and Tuesday I just added an extra karate class for beginners."

He wishes he could banish the admiration she shows him. He doesn't deserve it, he knows that better than anyone. "You work so hard. How do you still have time to volunteer for the church every day?"

"You make time, for the things you love." At least it isn't a long drive to the apartment complex they share. On the down side, the heater doesn't really start kicking in until they're halfway home, tires crunching steadily over fresh snow.

"Ploughs haven't come through yet. I'm sorry, I wouldn't have bothered you, but it's hell getting a taxi when it's this cold out."

"I don't mind. How's your younger sister? Still in the hospital?"

"I can't believe you remember that."

Stop looking at me like that. I'm not what you want. "I just wish the best for all you and yours. You're both in my prayers."

It's probably because he's preoccupied with wondering if he's going to find a drunken Shane on his doorstep, or trying to navigate the powdery white roads, or trying to figure out how to subtly hint to Deborah that there's no tree farther than him from the one she wants to be barking up, that he doesn't hear the sound until too late.

For a split second, Drake thinks he's lost control of the car, and it's gone slamming into a brick wall. Deborah screams, and he has just enough time to realize that if they'd hit something they'd have slowed down, or stopped moving, when whatever's grabbed them yanks the car sideways, sending them into a roll.

Then they hit a wall, with an absolute, final *crunch*. It's difficult to orient himself, but Drake thinks he's upside down, and not too badly damaged to keep living. He tastes blood, but that's probably just the inside of his mouth, bitten during the crash, and he blinks bleary eyes, focusing on the slender form of the woman in the passenger seat. "Deborah? You okay?"

"I—" She coughs, but nods. "I th-think so. What did we hit?"

Drake starts to answer, but at the surge of movement outside his shattered windows, his voice dries up into one word. "That."

The creature is massive, swelling to the size of a house, its shining black chitin the only thing he can see at this hour, in this light. More frightening than anything, it moves in total silence, its legs not even making noise as they touch the ground, and it rips the passenger-side door off its hinges with a single wrench of one arm.

Deborah doesn't scream. Her eyes are wide as dinner plates, and her breath is trembling in her lungs, but she seems to be beyond screaming. She's shuddering, and Drake doesn't wait for those arms—how many does it have?—to come down again. He yanks at the catch on his seat, collapsing it backward with a wrench of his back, and fumbles in the backseat for the long cloth-covered bundle he knows is back there, strapped in securely, never more than an arm's reach away.

For, you know, situations exactly like this.

His hand closes around the hilt, and he shuts his eyes on reflex at the usual blinding flash. Instantly, the minor cuts and bruises seem like nothing at all, the shaking he hadn't even noticed banished, and strength surges through him as he cleaves through the warped metal of the door, hacking himself an escape hole.

The damn thing moves silently, and that's not only creepy as all hell, it's dangerous too. It doesn't telegraph its moves, doesn't let him know where it's going, give any of the usual indicators that he sort of needs to be able to fight it.

"Drake!" Deborah screams, seeing one of the arms coming down towards her, eyes fixed on it rather than on him.

He vaults over the overturned car with a massive leap, arms

swinging down with sword in tow, hammering down at the outstretched appendage. It looks more like a tentacle than an arm with the way it moves, but the hard slippery shell shouldn't be that flexible, that's not *fair*.

"Dra—" Deborah starts to yell again, then stops, stunned, seeing him land on the other side of the car, shining broadsword in his hands. He aims for the outstretched arm, but the damn thing is fast, dodging to the side. At least he's bought Deborah a couple seconds. "Deborah! Get out of here, fast as you can!"

Usually, running away is the right choice for humans. For all the big talk of bravery in popular fiction through the ages, Drake knows very well that there are things in the world—most of them, really—that it's just better to run away from.

Whatever the hell this thing is, he's ninety nine percent sure it's one of them. "Hey!" he shouts, running around to the thing's other side, spreading his arms to present a bigger target, no matter how it strains his muscles to hold the broadsword one-handed. "You come here for me? I'm right here."

From this angle, he has a better view of the thing, and vehemently wishes he didn't. It's tall enough that the hunch of its back brushes against the streetlights, with a perfectly round, un-segmented body. The curve of its chitinous shell makes for a totally spherical body, shimmering sleek black in the streetlights, reflecting the red and green of the flashing stoplights in the intersection. The legs are another thing entirely, shooting up to hold that oddly round body ten or so yards above the ground, moving fluidly around as though only vaguely connected to the body proper.

Drake swallows hard. Whatever this thing is, it's nothing he's faced before. For a moment, he can't help the thought that it would be *really nice* to have a certain man at his back, guarding his weak side, or even just encouraging him while they pelt headlong into danger together, but he squashes that thought. He's been fine on his own for years now. And he's got the scars to prove it, he thinks sourly, and dodges just in time to avoid a swipe of those eerily silent legs.

Too late, Drake realizes that he's more hampered by the lack of sound than he'd thought. No matter how fast he avoids one arm, the thing has another coming at him, not even whistling through the air as it strikes him in the back. It fastens on to him, even through his clothes, and something sharp stabs him in the spine, slender as a needle's prick and infinitely more painful.

Far more disturbing, he feels another attack, more subtle, more dangerous, the kind of thing he hasn't felt in years, seeping into his body from that tiny stab wound. For a moment, everything is silence, and he can see his body from behind, a pathetic human thing, facing something a hundred times larger than himself, slowly going limp. The silence steals over everything, quieting the ever-present pain, the guilt, the anger that's so much a part of him it just feels like background noise.

Then, the sword in his hand blazes. The light shocks him, intensely, offensively bright, hurting him even in his spirit form, worse still to the spherical creature. It shrieks, a horrible soundless cry that reverberates through everything nearby, rattling his bones. He snaps back into his body with a shock, hand tingling where it grips his sword, and he spares a quick moment to send up a prayer of thanks.

It's the only polite response, after all.

Feeling oddly energized Drake leaps forward, launching himself with a fierce bellow as he swings, and has the satisfaction of hearing that arm break, shattered and torn by the sword's sharp edge.

He starts to grin, but stops. There's no one to grin at.

The creature shrieks again, yanking its severed arm back towards itself in obvious pain, scuttling awkwardly on its five remaining legs off to the side.

"I see now," Drake mutters, loud enough for the thing's benefit. "You're not some new import from Fae. You're not an escaped pet of some stupid mage. You're just a big ugly bug."

He can almost hear the jokes his own stupid mage would make—would have made, he reminds himself, and even having the thought makes him angry enough to leap at the bug again, scoring a long line down another thick arm, snarling savagely as oddly pink blood gushes forth.

It runs, dashing down the streets faster than a creature of that size should be able to, and Drake thinks for a second that it's all flailing limbs in pain, before he hears a breathy, high-pitched shriek.

The arm wrenches away from Deborah's back, something ephemeral and oddly blurry in a way real objects aren't, and Drake's heart clenches. He sees her drop, lifeless and uncaring, to the ground.

Drake sheathes the sword on his back, taking the time to at least prop Deborah's body up in the remains of the car, checking to see that yes, she still has a pulse.

"Don't worry," he promises, "I'll get it back. I'll make sure you don't have to live like this."

No matter who she is, what his personal feelings, she doesn't deserve this. No one does.

He straightens up, mutters, "Please, guide my feet," and takes off at a dead run, long legs carrying him through the unnaturally dark streets, courtesy of the broken streetlights.

Damned if he's going to let someone else lose a soul because of him.

First Interlude

Nine Years Earlier

Shane can't help but laugh as he tosses power around, swelling with the heady exhilaration of it, of feeling so *unstoppable*. "Finally," he calls, giddy under the thunderstorm that rages all around them, "you're putting up something like a fight!"

Drake grabs his shoulder, sheltered with him in the eye of the storm artificially created by Shane's shields. "Don't get cocky," he warns before slicing down one of Kaliga's minions, putting a sword through his chest and a bullet through his head when he reanimates in a flash of white. "He still might have another trick up his sleeve. Remember to kill him twice."

There's a big part of Shane that just wants to ask who cares, when no one can stop them, when no one's been able to even dent them for years.

Then, up on the hill, in the light of a flash of lightning, a figure tumbles to the ground. "Kaliga!"

"Go!" Drake shouts, shoving him hard in the back. "I'll hold them off here. Get him while he's summoning the next wave!"

"We're not getting paid nearly enough for this," Shane calls over his shoulder, winking.

"We're not getting paid at all for this! I took it pro bono!"

"You bastard, I'll give you pro bono!"

Drake just blows him a kiss.

After that it's all running and dodging, weaving past the obvious traps and the lurking armies, until Shane reaches the bedraggled figure of an emaciated yellow-and-red skinned figure on the hill, some creature of the underworld that's clawed itself up with an army and a name and a plan. "You know," Shane remarks, drawing back his hand for a final strike, "you take-over-the-world types never pay as well as people who kidnap a single child. What do you think that says about the world?"

Kaliga sneers at him, eyes at least twenty-five percent of his face, and screeches, "I will rain blood down upon—"

Shane swallows his distaste and lets fly, blasting the creature's head from its body to land in several tiny pieces. He hates it, killing with magic, killing at all, but there's no reasoning with Kaliga's people, whatever they are. They haven't existed in the world for long enough to name, only long enough to murder several town's worth of people in the Midwest.

He watches the corpse for long minutes, but Kaliga doesn't reanimate like the rest of his army. Wearily, Shane turns back to the valley, trudging down the hill to find Drake giving him a tired thumbs-up. "Good day's work."

"Yeah. Too bad we didn't make anything on it."

"Just think of it like we saved the lives of many future employers." Drake grins, flashing white teeth, and Shane can't help but smile along with him.

White flashes behind Drake, and Shane doesn't even have time to scream before Kaliga plays his last trick, a long blade reaching red through Drake's chest before Shane pumps him so full of destructive magic that he explodes.

Shane runs faster than humanly possible, hitting the ground without realizing he'd been airborne, managing to catch Drake before he falls. "Baby, baby, stop it, are you okay?"

Drake's hand twitches weakly toward his chest, an expression of startled shock on his face. "It's cold."

Shane tries to heal him, tries to summon the energy but he can't think, and he's drained after fighting all day, and this isn't supposed to happen. "Gonna fix you," he mutters, ignoring the fact that it's not working, that goddamn Kaliga must have used some cursed dagger he doesn't have time to figure out, because his spell isn't taking. He barely manages to slow the pulse of blood from the wound, seeping out and staining his fingers red and that's not helping when he's trying to concentrate.

Drake's eyes flutter a few times. "Shane."

"Shut up, don't you dare talk to me like you're dying, I'll kill you myself, baby, just shut up and let me *fix* you."

Even as he says the words, the tears start falling because it's not working. Nothing he does is helping, nothing is fixing him, and Shane's never felt so helpless in his life, watching Drake bleed to death under his hands. "I'm sorry, baby, I—don't, please, I'm gonna figure it out, just don't—"

Drake's lips twitch into a smile. "Worth it. It was worth it."

His eyes slide shut.

Before Shane can do something—the tattered thoughts in his mind run to blasting apart the whole countryside, or killing himself, or trying to pick himself up and continue when the last thing he loved in the world is gone—Drake freezes in his hands. He turns to ice in an instant, clear and cold as a white figure steps out of a sudden cyclone of ice.

Shane's blood goes cold, and not just because he's holding Drake's frozen body. He knows exactly who's come to see him in this godforsaken wasteland. "The Ice King, isn't it? I've killed a few of your men."

"And more of my creatures. You are a powerful mage, Shane Conell."

"Why are you here?"

Frozen lips thin, into what could generously be called a smile. "Because this is the greatest opportunity I am ever likely to get. Do you want to save him?"

Shane's heart constricts. Never in his life has he wanted so badly to unmake something that's happened, not even after the death of his family. "I can't. I tried. I lost him."

"He's not dead yet. Not quite. I can heal him, and give you power even far beyond what you have now."

Shane hesitates. A part of him wants to scream at himself for hesitating when Drake's about to *die*, could die at any second, but they haven't lived this long without learning to be suspicious of anyone who wants to help them. "Would he be truly healed? Not dependent continually on you for life, or trapped in a strange limbo, or suffering forever?"

"He would be exactly as he was in the instant before the blade cleft him," the Ice King clarifies. "No bindings, no bonds. He would be free, just as he was."

"And me?"

The creature's eyes narrow slightly. "I think you have some idea already."

They've fought the Ice King's vassals before, Shane and Drake. The men and women of the Frozen Court are powerful, but cold, long since devoid of humanity in exchange for whatever cheap trinkets the Ice King tossed their way.

Every part of Shane rebels, screaming in horror at the very idea, the thought of having body and soul enslaved to a cold, remorseless creature like this. "*No pacts,*" Drake's voice echoes in his mind. "*No deals. Nothing that binds us to anyone except each other.*"

But I can't be bound to you if you're dead.

I can't be anything if you're dead.

Drake's lifeless face looks peaceful, as if he's sleeping, and Shane is absolutely sick of being helpless. Most powerful mage in the world, and what does it get him? Couldn't save his family. Couldn't save his boyfriend. Can't save himself.

How long will he even last, without Drake to keep him grounded, keep him sane? He remembers the time before moving in next door to the Young household. He remembers the hate, the shame, the anger and sadness that had been his constant companions, knowing he was different, that he was probably responsible for his parents' deaths just by being *himself.*

Was it going to be like that from now on, without him?

Drake was wrong. It isn't worth it, not without Drake there. Wiping his face on one bloody hand, Shane nods. "Yes. Okay. You can have my soul if you fix him."

With the last feelings he's ever going to have, Shane looks down at Drake's sleeping face, then watches the ice melt, the wound close. Drake opens his eyes and grins, sitting up. "That was a close one, huh?"

Shane gives him a smile, the last one he'll ever feel. "Baby, you have no idea."

Then the Ice King rips away his soul.

Chapter Three

One of Shane's boots hits the ground before his car's wheels have entirely stopped spinning, crunching satisfyingly against the gravel. He shrugs on his coat, a thick leather jacket that has just about no effect on how much cold he feels, and buckles on his swordbelt, then checks his hair in the mirror. Huh. Black today. Maybe he was looking forward to this.

It does feel good, he supposes, to stretch his legs. It's been a week since the last time he left the Ice King's fortress, concealed under a wholesale illusion covering an obscure government-sounding office. Even then, he'd only left to get drunk and pass out at Drake's doorstep—or was that the time he'd crashed service? It's hard to remember the things that don't matter. Mostly it just feels cold.

He unclips the GPS from his windshield, palming the little device. He taps it with a finger, flicking it to life. "Hey. Where is he?"

"Turn left. In four hundred feet, turn right onto Seventeenth Street."

"Who the hell measures in feet anyway?" he grumbles, stuffing it into his pocket along with his hands, strolling off down the street.

"Turn left."

Shane pauses, then pulls the GPS out to scowl at it. It's a new model, and should be able to handle the spell he'd put on it for a year, at least. "You said turn right."

"Turn left," it repeats, stubbornly.

"Look, this isn't complicated. Find Roy. How many feet?"

"Your destination is on the left. Right. Left."

"Fucking piece of shit." Shane jabs at the buttons, succeeding in changing her voice to Arabic, then Japanese, then Dark Fae, which he's pretty sure wasn't included with the regular package at Radio World.

"Snearthen Asghar."

He's so preoccupied with snarling every Dark Fae curse he knows at the thing that he doesn't notice the men creeping up on him until the cold barrel of a gun presses against his temple.

"Your wallet and your keys. Don't turn around. Don't fucking look at me."

Oh, this man wants to be menacing. Shane tries, with limited success, not to smirk. "My keys?"

"You got a sweet ride." One of the men sneers, pressing closer to him. "Maybe you'd be a sweet ride too, huh, faggot?"

"Well, if you're offering."

The wandering hand freezes, then pulls back in obvious confusion. "What the fuck did you just say to me, shithead? You wanna eat lead?"

"Probably tastes better than your dick."

That does the trick. A thought from Shane freezes the hammer on the gun a split-second before it clicks, leaving one thug cursing at the damn thing as Shane moves, slamming the heel of his hand up into the second man's nose, hard enough to drive bone splinters into his brain.

"Cheap trick," he says with a shrug as the dying man collapses to the ground, twitching and bleeding from the nose and ears. "Effective, though. How about you, big man? You wanna bleed?"

The second thug tosses his useless gun to the ground, hands in the air. "N-no, man, I didn't—"

He doesn't bleed. Shane freezes him where he stands, an unguarded touch of his finger lowering the man's temperature to somewhere that he vaguely remembers from high school only registers on the Kelvin scale. "It's a cute conceit, that you can unfreeze someone," he remarks casually, shaking off the ice clinging to his finger. "They come back to life a hundred years later and wake up and say, 'hey, what did I miss?' Just like that, their heart starts beating again, and their flesh hasn't atrophied at all. Why don't you tell me how that works out for you?"

On second thought, there's no reason to leave that kind of evidence behind, and there's enough of his power in the death to make a certain mortician of his acquaintance ask awkward questions. He stoops down, picks up the "broken" gun, and unfreezes the hammer. "This is cleaner. Well. Not for you."

The shot is loud, as is the sound of the man shattering into a hundred thousand pieces, landing in frozen bits around the alley. Shane flicks a piece off his jacket, then pulls out his GPS, shaking it. "Gonna work now?"

"Snearthen Asghar."

"If you say so."

He sets off at a trot, jogging left around a corner, only to see his target lying unconscious on top of a dumpster. "Dumbass. Wake up, Roy." He accompanies his words with a flick of cold wind, and Roy yelps as he wakes, patting himself down.

"Boss? What are you doing?"

"Tracked you. Shit, how long did it take to wipe the floor with you?"

Roy groans, sitting up and squirming around, grabbing at his own back. "I don't know, boss. Ten seconds? It's, uh, bigger than I thought. Tried to suck out my soul."

Shane laughs. "I hope that's the only trick it has. Turn over."

"I—"

"Turn the fuck over, I'm gonna track its signature."

It's the work of a few annoying moments to feed the sensory magic he gets from the impression in Roy's back into the GPS, and the thing stutters hesitantly to life. "Get that?" he asks the spell, pressing a few buttons for the hell of it.

"Snearthen Heirge."

"Cool." He tosses Roy his keys, already following the directions. "Get the fuck out of here. This is obviously too big for you."

Roy glares at him, but it's more wounded pride than anger. "I could have caught you in the rankings."

"Sure. Out you get, I've got to Sneathen Heirge. Tell the King he'll have its head by tonight."

"You're a fucking bastard, boss."

And you wouldn't have been anywhere near me in the rankings if I'd bothered hunting a single thing in the last two years. There's something to fucking brag about.

Sure, it's *nice* being on top in the rankings, like it's nice having the penthouse room, the bank account with nine figures, the cars and the amulets and the place of honor at all the feasts and orgies. Like everything else, it gets boring after a while.

Doesn't mean he wants to give all that to *Roy*, though.

"Sneathen Vrache."

"Watch your language." He turns obediently right (well, northeast, the Dark Fae have an oddly precise sense of direction-giving) and stops in his tracks.

"Imschalle Trezimon."

"No shit," Shane mutters, staring up at the creature. It looms over him, a towering thing of spindly legs (two injured, he files away) and shiny black body, wreathed in eerie silence, and all five of its eyes swivel down to stare at him.

Unbidden, a smirk steals over his lips, because damned if this isn't the first interesting thing he's seen in years. Oh, this is gonna be fun.

He starts to run, uncloaking his power as he does, the constant sensation of being tamped down vanishing at last from the back of his mind. It races through him, the magic making his veins sing, his hands tingle, his eyes flicker. He runs towards the creature and then up one of the alley walls, hardly noticing the way gravity warps itself for the turn, and unsheathes his sword as he goes.

One of the Soul-Thief's arms lashes out at him, and he dodges midair, a gust of icy wind catching him before he falls, bearing him up swiftly enough to wrap a hand around one of the Soul-Thief's legs.

That's a mistake.

The thing's arms are coated in some kind of acid, some gelatinous gloop that starts burning as soon as he touches it, and he doesn't even retain the presence of mind to swear in an interesting language as he drops it, collapsing to the ground. "Mother*fucker*, I'm going to kill you for that!"

The acid isn't just painful. Even as he watches his fingers burn, melt away, corroded by the sticky stuff. His hand withers as the flesh burns away in searing pain, skin falling to the ground, muscles and blood withering to bone.

Wow. That actually hurts.

For a second, it almost feels good, a flare of pain when he's been cold, unfeeling for so long, but shit, he can't let this go on, no matter how interesting the sensation.

His eyes blaze, briefly lighting up the alley with blue-white light, and his hand covers itself in ice, hardening, dulling the pain to the point of the usual frozen ache he feels, well, everywhere. He flexes his hand, hearing the ice chip and crack, little pieces of acid-riddled ice flaking off to land on the alley floor. It'll require a healing—fuck, with how much his hand hurts, it might require a *re-making*—but for now, he can make do with the ice hand, the decay halted by the quick freeze.

Shane bares his teeth and lets loose with a blast of raw power that knocks the Soul-Thief off its many legs, bowling it over to land against a fire escape. It scrabbles madly at the iron to haul itself upright. "Sorry," Shane snaps, patience waning drastically after the pain, "bet that stings like a bitch. Hell, if you're not more polite, I'll get a can of Raid."

The Soul-Thief flips over with speed that really isn't fair, feet clawing at the asphalt with a screech that burns the ear.

With the hand that's mostly ice Shane draws his sword, transferring it to the still-living flesh of his right hand. "Should've stuck to wherever the fuck you came from. Can you even talk?"

The thing screams at him, but it's wordless, at least as far as he can tell. "Guess not. Maybe if you'd been less of a bitch I'd have just squashed you with a giant shoe, but you're just asking for pain."

One of the arms flails at him, something that looks like a needle-sharp stinger extended, and Shane moves so fast the world blurs in front of him, spinning around and striking out with his sword arm, shaving a long slab of armor from the arm, enjoying the way the thing writhes and thrashes as the sword turns every part it touches to ice. "Yeah, well, I don't like what you did to my arm either. Live with it, bitch. Or bastard."

Probably not a line of questioning he wants to pursue, really.

Putting far, far to the side the question of whether the Soul-Thief has a dick or not, Shane twists his sword, wrenching it free, and the suddenly brittle arm of the thing shatters into two pieces. Not as effective as it is on humans, then, where a single nick is enough to turn the entire body to ice. That's all right. It's no fun without a challenge, and the Soul-Thief is down to three arms.

"Still one up on me," Shane grunts, narrowly avoiding another swat of the stinger. If it hadn't been for the way it knocked Roy unconscious, he'd have been tempted to let it try and zap him, just to hear it freak out in surprise. Then again, the noises it's making are overwhelming enough as it is.

He flexes his newly constructed ice hand, wiggling it around until it more or less settles into the shape of his actual hand, or what his hand would be if it weren't currently so much damaged bone and sinew.

As a test, Shane tries to freeze the Soul-Thief with a sheer act of will. It's more difficult than touching something, than letting the cold inside him spill out for a change, but it's not exactly hard either.

He takes a deep breath, easier said than done while he dodges three acidic limbs whipping around at the speed of sound. Mentally, he forms the power into a lance, a spreading, infectious thing impregnated with all the ice he can muster, and hurls it at the broad center of the great teetering thing.

It has about the same effect as throwing a ping-pong ball at a meteorite.

"Okay." Shane's voice wavers a little, his eyes blazing again, hand gripping the hilt of his sword more tightly than ever. "You want to fucking play? Let's see you dance."

He drops the tip of his sword to the asphalt, and ice spills out, slicking the ground for a good three hundred yards in every direction. The Soul-Thief slips, legs skittering madly, and fails to catch itself, toppling over to hit the ice with a *crack* of shattering… body? Ice? Hard to tell.

Shane dashes forward, feeling the wind rip past him even for such a short distance, feet never slipping as he runs forward, sword outstretched, to deal the final blow to the downed, doomed creature.

His sword meets something hard with a blaze of light, so bright it sends him flying back, one arm thrown over his eyes. "Bastard!" he chokes out, blinking furiously as he twirls the sword one-handed. "Playing possum, huh? I'll—"

His vision clears, and the next words die in his throat as he sees exactly what's interspersed itself between him and his prey. His mouth goes abruptly dry, and he stammers, "D-Drake, what—"

If he had to put a name to the emotion on Drake's face, he'd be hard put to think of anything besides weary disappointment. Drake winces, but nods. "Shane."

I was doing something. Probably something important. "You look good. I like that shirt. Want to rip it off you."

"For the love of God, can't you think of anything except—"

"You?" Pain flares behind the smile spreading across Shane's face, and he welcomes it, embraces it as the best thing he's felt in years. "Probably not. I don't try. Say, can we get back to this in like twenty seconds? I've got a mark to bag."

Drake shifts, and just like that, Shane knows, just knows that there's trouble. "I can't let you kill it."

The smile curves, turns less nice, and Shane's eyebrows raise. "Let me? You think you can stop me?"

"Don't do this."

Shane saunters forward, a wicked glint in his eye. He leans forward, enough so his breath will be chill against Drake's ear as he hisses, "So *stop* me."

Drake telegraphs his moves by a mile, always has. He's fast, sure, but not in the same league as Shane, making it laughably easy for him to dance out of the broadsword's range. "That's the problem with being a big man swinging a big sword," he taunts, as Drake pulls back his arms for another swing. "All your momentum is—"

Just as he slides smoothly away from the next swing, Drake kicks out, a powerful sweep of his leg that takes Shane square in the hip, slamming him back into the half-broken fire escape the Soul-Thief had scrabbled down earlier. The iron bars drive into his ribs, his stomach, and had he been a lesser man, would have broken a *lot* that he can't afford to break right now.

It's a little hard to stay focused on why he needs to capture the Soul-Thief, why he *needs* to bring it down when the very thing that he wants is standing right in front of him, kicking him in the chest for good measure. For a second, Shane just grins, tasting blood. "Missed you too."

Drake brings his sword up again, and this time Shane sees it for the decoy that it is, sees the muscles bunch in his side and thigh. He throws out his hand, and the surge of power smacks into Drake's weight-bearing leg, sending him spinning off over a patch of still-frozen ground.

Shane wipes his mouth on the back of his hand—cut lip from the fall, no problem—and gets to his feet, unable to keep the grin off his face. "If you're a good boy and hold still, this can end without—"

The sword blazes, that *damn sword*, he always forgets to account for it, and Shane throws up a hand over his eyes, following instinctively with a shield of power with his other hand, just in time to feel Drake smash against it. He lowers his hand, still blinking away the stars, and sheathes his sword. "You want to fight, big man? I can go all fucking night. Which city block should we tear up first, huh?"

"There are people living in those buildings."

Shane laughs. "Yeah, but you're the one who gives a shit about that. Come on. I'll let you have the first shot." He nods towards the sword in Drake's hands, lifting his eyebrows in challenge. "Think that thing would work on me?"

"Of course not. It only works on—"

"Shit that isn't human," Shane finishes, smirking. He walks forward, eyes locked on Drake, slowly extending his hand. "Want to see if I still bleed?"

"Shane."

"You wonder, don't you? Or maybe you don't think about me at all. Not like I think about you." He keeps advancing, feet crunching over the ice, power crackling around his hands.

"Shane, don't. We don't have to fight."

"You gonna stop me from killing my mark?"

Drake swallows hard, but nods. "I have to."

Within a few feet, then inches, Shane manages to look down at Drake even though he's got an inch of height on him. "Then stop me," he murmurs, drawing his hand back for a blast that will probably level the whole block.

Drake kisses him.

The power flares in Shane's hand, then arcs back into his body, setting his nerves alight with electricity, contorting his spine into an arch of gasping shock as Drake's mouth closes over his, hard and wet and wanting. That thing in his chest, that spark of pain in the middle of the ever-present cold, flares white-hot, a searing agony that brings actual tears to Shane's eyes, and god, if anything's ever felt so good he doesn't remember it.

For a moment, the pain overwhelms him until he feels a little like himself again, like the words, *Nice try, baby, you think I'm that easy?* are on the tip of his tongue, an easy teasing smile, a hand twined gently with his. With the taste of Drake so strong on his tongue, the hard planes of his body pressed against him, it's easy to pretend that they're not in a filthy alley but in their old apartment, practice blades tossed to the ground during a sparring session where they just couldn't keep their hands off each other, panting and sweaty and *hungry*.

Maybe he's not the only one who feels it.

Shane's back hits the brick wall again as Drake shoves him, pressing him there with all his weight, and no matter how strong and lithe Shane is Drake's always been a huge guy, would be intimidating if not for the open honest kindness of his features. The weight of him feels *good*, something immediate and searingly hot when everything's been ice for so long. Then they're both grabbing, yanking and tearing at clothing, totally absorbed in the fervent need for each other that's never gone away, not really.

Drake's hand comes up to fist in Shane's hair, his eyes intensely blue as he yanks his head back. "You hard?"

Shane lets out a strangled noise, hips rutting forward involuntarily against Drake's thigh, showing him just how much. "Yes. For you. Please."

He sees it, that wavering, desperate look in Drake's eyes that he knows better than anyone in the world, and it makes him tremble. His legs spread, his mouth goes dry, and he nods quickly, muttering, "Do it, it's okay, I want it, it's me."

Dear, sweet, honest, kind, *saintly* Drake. He's always been the sort of man to make the simpering ladies at his church swear that it's possible to have a man without a mean side, it's possible to be human without having an ounce of darkness in the soul.

In his less sober moments, Shane's always wanted to dare those women to try fucking Drake and see if they still believe that afterwards.

Big hands close around his hips, pulling him close just to slam him back into the wall again, the impact driving the breath from his lungs. Drake's mouth is hungry on his, biting sharply into his lip, down his neck, hoisting him up careless of the brick scraping Shane's back. "You like to talk so much," Drake growls, hands tight enough to leave bruises on even Shane's hips. "Open your mouth. Beg me. Like a whore."

There's nothing fake, nothing artificial about the way Shane whimpers, hands splayed over Drake's chest as he moans, "Please. Fuck me. Need you, please, baby."

Drake's hands catch Shane's wrists, forcing them over his head and holding them there with one big hand. "Want you to suck me off first," Drake breathes, every muscle in his body quivering with suppressed emotion, "but I can't wait. Spread your legs."

He yanks Shane around, grabbing him and arranging him the way he wants him, like a compliant rag doll, until his legs are wrapped around Drake's waist, his hands pinned above his head. Drake shifts forward, rubbing his cock up against Shane's hole, teasing, pressing just a little, and Shane's mouth falls open. A surge of need shoots through him—*need it want it more than anything missed this missed you need it oh GOD put it in me*—and he's not even sure how much he says out loud, every fiber of his body squirming around to try and slam himself down, to have it again after so long. "Please!"

"Do that thing or it'll hurt. Me," Drake adds, coppery eyes gone dark. "We both know you like it when it hurts."

It's the work of a bare thought to slick Drake's cock, the only spell he can ever think of when he's like this, horny and desperate and needing, twisting against the hold on his hands, trying to fuck himself down on that perfect thick cock, something he knows better than his own hand, even after all these years apart.

Drake's not gentle when he thrusts in, and he doesn't go slow, rough and brutal as he fucks Shane into the brick wall, spreading and stretching him with every snap of his hips. Shane lets out stupid, embarrassing sounds, little breathy shrieks because it's too much, no matter how many times they've done this it's always too big, always too much, always too hard.

And he always loves it.

Drake's free hand wrenches his hair back, then slides down to close around his throat, feeling his blood pulse in time with every pounding thrust.

It's good, a different kind of pain than he's used to, and with every crash of Drake's hard body against his he feels, he *remembers* the things that usually slip away from him, carried off by the apathy. He remembers what it was like to be thrown over their old sturdy table, fucked until he came over the glass panel, then held down by his hair until he licked it all up. He remembers the night they broke the bed, when he hadn't been able to sit down for three days because he'd refused to heal himself. He remembers getting fucked in the bedroom, the shower, the kitchen, the living room, over the couch, against every wall, on the floor like a dog.

Shane writhes under Drake's big hands and the punishing thrusts of his cock, slamming himself down no matter how much it hurts, his own cock hard and leaking between them. "F-fuck, I—"

"Don't talk."

Shane shuts up.

He's so full he aches, that he's reduced to a trembling, twitching thing, clenching down on the demanding length filling him, pressing inside him so right, stealing his breath and making him see stars.

"Gonna come for me?"

Shane nods frantically, hands twisting to try and slip Drake's hold, to wrap around himself, but if anything the fingers only close tighter around his wrists. "Slut. You're really aching for my cock."

That's all it takes, filthy words falling from such a gentle-looking mouth. Shane cries out, every muscle gone tight, his legs clenching hard, writhing so much he scrapes his own back against the wall and doesn't *care*. Every little pain adds to the wave that crashes over him, making him spill hot and wet between them.

Just like that, just at the look in Drake's eyes, predatory and focused, he knows he's going to come inside. With a curse and a groan, Drake slams forward, burying himself to the hilt and it's too much, *too much* on top of everything, and Shane can't stop himself from whining by the time Drake finally goes still, slick hot fluid filling him even more.

The countdown starts in Shane's head, and he nearly starts crying. Seventeen seconds. That's the longest it's ever taken for them to remember what they'd been fighting about before, for the first insult or apology or rueful chuckle.

He makes it to sixteen before Drake pulls out, slowly disengaging with a look of the most complete shame on his face. "I—I shouldn't have."

"It's okay." God, it's lingering, the feeling that he's himself again, that he can have feelings besides resentment and aching, bitter longing. "I need to kill it, though. It's not about rankings."

Drake's eyebrows snap together, and he tilts his head curiously as he fumbles for his clothes. "It's not? Then what?"

"It's a prize." He swallows hard, almost not wanting to get Drake's hopes up, but… "If I bag it, he gives me my soul back."

Drake freezes so suddenly Shane almost checks to make sure he hasn't nicked the other man with his sword. "Is this a trick?" he demands, yanking his shirt over his head.

"If it is, it's on me." Shane spreads his hands, shrugging. "I don't give a shit about the rankings anymore, Drake. I don't give a shit about anything except you."

"Don't. You can't."

"Just because the goddamn Ice King's sitting on my soul doesn't mean a damn thing to me," Shane hisses, only now putting his own clothes on, flexing the new ice hand in disapproval. "All I know is that all my feelings were supposed to be gone nine years ago, and it still hurts to see you. Always. So you tell *me* what that means."

"I can't. Maybe if you hadn't sold your soul in the first place."

"Can we not start that again?" It's not angry, not really, just a pleading question, and Shane sidles forward to nuzzle down into the other man's chest. "Don't wanna fight. Just want you."

"Can't let you kill it. It stole my friend's soul."

"Oh. Well, if that's all, I'll just get it out. Then I can kill it, yes?"

Something that could be a smile hovers around Drake's lips, and he nods before it can take hold. "All right. You sure you can?"

"You think I can't? Watch me." In all honesty, Shane has no idea if he can, or what the process would even entail. Then again, what's the worst that can happen? He'll probably wind up killing the girl, and Drake probably doesn't care *that* much about her.

He can always apologize once he has his soul back. Then it'll actually mean something.

"Almost got it." Fuck, this is a lot of trouble to go to just to keep one stupid girl from dying. "If I can just—"

The girl's presence vanishes, slipping through Shane's mental grasp as if evaporating into a wisp of smoke. He curses, reaches for her again, but there's nothing, less than nothing, as if she'd never been. "Lost her," he admits, not terribly broken up about it.

"That's not all."

Shane opens his eyes to ask what the fuck Drake means by that, and it turns into a barrage of curses in every language he knows at the sight of the slippery, damaged, extremely empty alley.

"What the *fuck*? Where did it go?"

Drake grabs his shoulder, so tight he'll leave bruises. "You tell me. Where did you send it?"

"Me? Send it?" Shane swats away the hand, breaking the big man's grip with a whack on the wrist. "I didn't send it anywhere. I was trying to save some stupid mortal bitch that got herself snatched, but—"

"Where did it go?"

Just because Drake's being annoying, Shane punches him,

catching him hard on the cheekbone with his ice hand. "Blame me for goddamn everything. You sit here and pray or something. I'm gonna go find this piece of shit."

He stalks off, looking for something clear enough to take an imprint of, finding nothing but rocks and debris. Grimacing, he lets his hand melt onto the ground, trying to at least take a mental tracking of the Soul-Thief from the marks the acid had left on his flesh, but it's no use. The ice's work is long since done, eradicating all the acid from his skin.

"Jesus! Your hand!"

Shane shrugs, tapping his fingers against each other, hearing the bones click. It's an odd sensation, long since frozen past pain. "When we find it, don't touch its arms. Probably the body too, but I didn't feel like checking."

"You have to get to a doctor! Doesn't that hurt?"

"Nah. Feels kind of good."

For such a big man, Drake can move quietly when he wants to, and Shane doesn't realize he's moving until warm hands close over the tattered remnants of his hand. That hurts, that sore little pain in his gut that he associates with *Drake*, with wanting so badly he can't even breathe, can't think of anything except the fact that he'd had Drake, had him for years, and can't get him back. "Can you fix it?"

"Maybe. Haven't tried."

"Try."

"Later. After I catch it." He curls his fingers as best he can, the bits of muscle twitching uselessly. "If I do. If I get it back. I know it's a long shot, but if I do—"

Drake kisses him. Not to shut him up, not hard and needing like last time, but a gentle brush of his lips, warm and soft. "Of course."

"Sentimental idiot." The ice forms under Drake's hands, slow and sticking this time instead of hardening, fastening onto his flesh and rebuilding it as he stands. He laughs, wincing as it tickles. "Reminds me of that maggot thing. The one who offered to pay us in health?"

"God. I'd almost forgotten about that." Drake's grin is rueful, even as his eyes are fixed on the grotesque spectacle of Shane's arm regrowing itself. "I thought you were going to cry."

"What, just because a cow-sized larvae was chewing off all my dead skin cells? Give me a little credit. It just tickled, that's all." He licks his lips, then offers, "I can't get a good hit on it here. I was thinking of hitting up the old places, if you want…"

"Yeah. Okay."

Drake's always been unreadable, even at the best of times. Even as a skinny teenager he had that serious face ready to drop into place at a moment's notice, even before they'd come home to find his parents and siblings dead in their beds.

Before, back when everything was good, Shane had respected that, respected Drake's privacy. Now, he doesn't give a shit. "Why? You want to help me, or you afraid I'll kill your friend before you can stop me?"

Drake sheathes his sword. "Can't it be both?"

Chapter Four

It makes sense to go the The Symposium first. It's the most well-known coffee house and bar in the community, serving the strangest customers that even downtown Sunrise City can muster up. It's the perfect place to go to relax, to uncloak, to let the natural skin color show, and to gather information.

That doesn't mean Drake has to like it.

"Been here recently?"

"No." He's not nervous, he reasons with himself. It's just… awkward.

"When was the last time?"

"Nine years. Or close enough."

Shane probably doesn't know how creepy he is now, to anyone that knew him *before*, least of all to Drake, who knew him best of all. He remembers effortlessly how alive Shane's face, his eyes, had been. A comment like that would have drawn a response, something guilty-curious-interested-ashamed-mocking-amused, because Shane's always been one to feel a million things at once. Now, he just nods. "All right. Let's get in there and see what we get. And then we'll find the Soul-Thief and you can fuck me again."

"That all you can think about?" The words come easily to his lips, not condescending but from long habit, even now.

Shane's mouth turns up at the corners as he answers, as usual,

"Only thing worth mentioning. Come on."

There's always a sense of relief upon entering The Symposium, something palpable and contagious. A little group of Waterfae sits in the corner, veils draped over the chairs, conversing excitedly in Bubblespeak. The tendrils of their hair wave gently as they move, sometimes reaching to entwine with each other in blue-green waves, making the fae roll their eyes as they reach for special combs. Two amateur mages with probably a sneeze worth of power each sit at a booth wearing too much eyeliner to ever be taken seriously, looking around in wide-eyed wonder, breaking the no-staring-if-you-want-to-keep-your-eyeballs rule. A mixed-bag group of Earthsprites, bounty hunters and Inferna play a dice game on the floor, arguing with the dice when they keep siding with the Inferna. A few more grizzled folk of indeterminate species and persuasion look them over as they enter, trying to decide if they pose a threat. One or two, a couple faces Drake remembers well, actually swear out loud at the sight of them. He hears the murmur go up, passing from mage to sprite to fae, that the Champion and the Vassal have entered.

It's silent by the time they reach the last step, even the dice falling quiet after the latest argument. Eyes of every color and shape fix on the pair of men, narrowing in distrust, in curiosity, occasionally in fear. Drake nods at a couple women he used to know, back from the old days. They don't nod back.

Shane surveys the surroundings, flexing his mostly-regrown hand, not terribly far from the hilt of his sword. "Quiet night. Maybe we can change that."

Silence greets his words.

"No? You're gonna hurt my feelings."

One of the Waterfae snorts at that, and her comrades shush her violently, huddling together in anxiety. A nervous people, Waterfae, Drake remembers not unfondly.

He clears his throat. "We're looking for the Soul-Thief. Big black bug, pissing a lot of people off. Corrosive skin, stingers, moves in total silence. Anyone seen anything like that?"

No one moves.

Just as Drake's about to thank them for their time, he feels a twitch of power from Shane next to him, lashing out into the crowd. "Oh," he murmurs, quiet as a whisper, still heard perfectly well over the ringing silence, "Someone knows. Stand up, pretty thing. I can feel you lying to me."

"That's not allowed in here." A bounty hunter, hard-voiced and craggy-faced, stands up between Shane and the direction he's staring in. "I don't know who the hell you think you are, but you can't just—"

One of the hunters at his table grabs him by the arm, yanking him back into his seat. Even at this distance Drake can hear a harsh whispered conversation taking place as Shane laughs unkindly. "You must be new. Sorry, you reminded me, I didn't introduce myself."

"Shane, don't!"

Drake's yell is too late, and a lance of ice lashes out from Shane's outstretched hand, arcing towards the hunter faster than the eye can track, making unerringly for his heart. Only a split-second lunge keeps him from being impaled, and the lance continues right through the wall, leaving a ragged hole through which daylight peeks in.

A couple of the cloaked figures hiss—probably Darkfae, poor things, Drake thinks in sympathy—before someone blocks the hole, walling out the light. The smirk on Shane's face is sinuous, dangerous, and he purrs, "For those of you to whom I haven't introduced myself, I'm Shane Conell, First Vassal of the Ice King. This is Drake Young, Champion of the Church."

"You don't have to sound so damn sarcastic."

"Just be glad I didn't use air quotes. Anyone in here see my bug?" After another moment of silence, Shane pulls out his wallet, of all things. "Look, I can feel that someone's lying. Anyone like bribery? How about a hundred thousand dollars? American money, not Ice Chips. Anyone want to be rich?"

From the back of the bar, one tiny voice says, "I-I might have seen."

A nearby cloaked figure hisses, "Shut up, idiot!"

"Don't tell me what to do! I saw it!" A little man, no more than three feet tall, stands up and scratches his nose. "I saw it, Vassal." He eyes the wallet, obviously wanting what's inside, but not daring to come any closer.

Shane stalks over to him, deliberately counting out more money than Drake's ever seen in one place, holding it in his outstretched hand. "Talk."

The little man licks his lips, turning an odd mottled blue color, and Drake places him as Charmelae, or at least half. To have ventured above the surface, this one must be brave indeed. "I-I saw a woman who—"

Drake feels it the second before it happens, tackling Shane to the ground as he yells, "Down!"

The blast that hits isn't height-specific, though, and lying in a tangle on the floor does them no good when it hits. The blast is soundless, a thing of impact instead of heat or fire, and washes over the bar in a torrent of *something* as bodies hit the ground. He turns Shane onto his back, intending only to check him for injuries, and hisses out a sharp breath at the sudden arousal that courses through him, surprising and inappropriate and *strong*.

"Oh," Shane says slowly, shaking his head to clear it as Drake tries to remember why it's a good idea to keep his hands to himself. "Yeah. Okay. That's gonna be Astra."

"What's Astra?" Drake asks, eyes never leaving Shane's body, focused only on the way his hips twitch upward, shifting needy and sinuous underneath him.

He's not the only one feeling it. He can see Shane's eyes wandering down his body, hovering at his groin, and Shane lets out a groan as he mutters, "Stupid bitch of a teenager who thinks she's tough shit."

"Say that to my face."

Shane wrenches his eyes from the front of Drake's jeans to a spot over his shoulder, sighing. "I'd rather tell you to take off your fucking spell or I'll rip your face off your skull and shove it into your—"

"That's enough," Drake says firmly, glaring down. He twists around, and stifles the urge to groan himself.

The girl standing there, hand on a cocked hip, hair dyed a startling shade of bubblegum pink, can't be more than sixteen, and she's obviously *rebelling*. Piercings stud her ears, nose, and eyebrows, and the nose of what's obviously a hummingbird tattoo peeks out from her low-slung waistband. On top, she wears little more than a bra, no matter the chill of the weather, and her shoes are sandals. Platform sandals, no less.

She smirks, and the sheer emptiness of it tells him instantly that this is another of Shane's underlings, vassals that don't come anywhere near him in power, but constantly attempt to overtake him in the rankings anyway. Usually Drake only finds out about it because in trying to best him and each other, they consistently destroy large chunks of the city, sometimes leaving many people dead. He's fought a few of them, gone toe-to-toe and never found them any real difficulty, far from being in the same weight class as a mage like Shane.

Then again, maybe this one's got more power than he gives her credit for after all. Everywhere he looks, he can see people lying on the ground, looking shellshocked and confused, some of them wrestling with the impulse to simply jump on each other and start rutting. A couple of them look close to blows, and Drake demands, "What did you do in here?"

"It's a stupid spell," Shane mutters, but the girl cuts him off.

"It's a really *good* spell," she snaps, folding her arms in a transparent attempt to push up her breasts, something that has little to no effect on either Drake or Shane. "I made it up myself."

He hears Shane snort, and has to agree. "Miss, I don't know

who told you that was an original idea, but I'm pretty sure there have been lust spells around since the turn of the century. Shit, it's the first thing any new mage tries when they're a teenager." It's way too easy to remember Shane's experiments with exactly that, back before it had become so obvious that neither of them needed, would ever need, such a thing.

"Whatever, this one's good. And it has range. And punch." She smirks, looking around in satisfaction. "The best part is, the more you try to distract your mind, the more your body reacts. Cool, huh?"

"It's stupid and you're dead." Shane moves to strike, but Drake expects the motion this time, moves in enough time to hold Shane's wrists down to the ground before he can lash out with a bolt of ice. Even that much contact is too much, and it nearly burns when they touch. It's too easy to remember the man Shane used to be, and god, he's still lovely, with that glossy dark hair against his pale skin, the sharp-edged features, prominent cheekbones, sinfully full plush lips. That's all the same, oddly the same, because while Drake looks every day of his thirty-five years, Shane hasn't aged in a decade. Frozen, Drake's mind supplies, even as his hands urge to just wander a bit.

Astra strolls past them, picking up the little man from a pile of the Waterfae who are either more susceptible to the spell than the rest of the patrons, or just see no reason not to drop trow in public. She holds him aloft in one hand, asking sweetly, "Where's the Soul-Thief? Tell me the truth and you can put your face in my boobs."

The little man looks around, vaguely panicking, looking for all the world as if he'd far rather have the money Shane was tossing around earlier. Nevertheless, he stammers, "Saw a w-woman who summoned it. She led it around like it was a pet by some jewel thing on a bracelet. They ran off South, on the lake side of Downtown!"

Astra drops him, stopping on her way to the door only to lean down and press a kiss to Shane's cheek. "Later, boss. But, you know, not. Because you won't be my boss anymore. So just...later."

She blows out the door, leaving it rocking off its hinges, vanishing into the early morning. A few Darkfae shriek again, this time abandoning the bar in favor of a nice hole in the ground, leaving few traces of their presence.

"I'm actually gonna wait to kill her," Shane remarks, hips rubbing up firmly against Drake's thigh. "I'm gonna wait until I get my soul back, because I want it to really be fun."

"You don't like killing. Not when you're you." It's getting more and more difficult to think through the spell, and every time he tries, it just makes him harder, just makes him ache.

"Really? Huh. I'd kind of forgotten that. Fuck me."

"It's the damn spell. Can you get rid of—"

"Yeah." Shane smirks, licking his lips. "But I won't."

"Dammit."

"Blasphemous talk from a man of God."

"This could be *dangerous*. There are Inferna here."

"Yeah? Wonder what their cocks are like. Maybe I'll find out."

"If you dare—"

"What?" Shane gets up into his face, lips a hairsbreadth from Drake, and it's impossible not to want to kiss him, to bruise those pretty lips. "You gonna tell everyone I'm yours? You gonna claim me again, big man? Everyone in here knows you threw me away. Go on, claim me."

"I can't." Not that he doesn't want to.

Behind Shane, he can see a couple of the bounty hunters grab one of the poser mages, see one of the Waterfae writhing on a few slithery appendages, and curses under his breath. "I fucking hate magical orgies and you know it."

"Spell only lasts until we come. All of us, and I bet there's a few people here with pretty fantastic endurance. Wonder how long it takes to make an Earthsprite come?"

Drake can't really deny how hard he is now, not with the way he's rutting down, urgent, needy, gripping Shane's hips and holding him. "Please—"

"I'll end the spell if you let me suck you off."

That's all the flimsy justification he needs, and Drake scrambles to his feet, yanks himself out and tangles a hand in silky black hair." Fine," he mutters, "but no one better turn into a centaur this time."

Shane's got to be just as bad off as he is, given the way he dives forward, sucking on Drake's cock with a slurping groan, taking it into his mouth with such hungry abandon it raises a shiver on his spine. Somehow, he always expects Shane's body to be as cold as his heart now, but it isn't. He's hot to the touch, always has been, and it's searing and wet and perfect inside his mouth.

"Miss when your hair was red. Looked so hot on you." He can remember the way it glinted in the sun streaming through the window of their apartment, fiery red and almost alive, always so soft to the touch. He remembers playing with it in the mornings, waking Shane like that, seeing his sleeping face settle into a gentle smile.

"You love sucking cock, don't you?" His voice comes out soft, but he knows Shane can hear him, even over the noise in the rest of the room. It's strange, having people who can see them, but damned if it's going to make him stop when Shane's swallowing his cock, slick tongue dragging up the underside, teeth catching just a little bit against the head, just the way Drake loves it. "You remember waking me up like this, you little pervert? Go on, take more. Get my cock down your throat where you obviously want it."

He jerks on Shane's hair, hips thrusting forward until he sees tears streaming down those pretty pale cheeks, then slamming the last inch of it in, down his throat until he can feel Shane's nose pressing against his abdomen. God, it feels good to see him struggling, to see him hard and writhing against his own hand, even as he shudders and sobs around the thick length stretching out his mouth.

"Perfect cocksucking whore." The words come back too easily, no matter that they don't feel right now, not now that he's ostensibly working for the Good Guys. It's far too easy to remember how good it feels to just grab Shane and *fuck him*, to screw him into whatever available flat surface he can find, to rough him up a bit until he's trembling and twitching.

A couple of the bounty hunters, the ones who'd recognized them earlier, drift over from their own coupling, eyeing Shane with undisguised contempt and even more poorly-hidden lust. One of them, a human Drake thinks might be called Jimmy Dego, reaches over and grabs Shane's ass.

"Watch it," Drake growls, but the men don't listen to him. Hands slide around and yank off the Vassal's designer jeans, tossing them to the ground. Drake's hands tighten in Shane's hair enough that he hears sloppy choking noises, and he nearly grabs for his sword before remembering.

He's not Shane's boyfriend.

He's not Shane's lover.

Hell, he has less right to Shane than the bounty hunters, because they've never rejected Shane, never slammed their doors on him when he turned up begging and drunk and desperate in the middle of the night.

Instead of marking his claim like he wants to, Drake pulls out of Shane's mouth, looking down at him. He doesn't say anything, even as Jimmy Dego laughs and licks one of his fingers, sliding it into Shane's ass.

Drake could cheerfully kill him.

He holds Shane's empty eyes, asking quietly, "Do you want me to do something about this?"

That fucking smirk.

It slides across Shane's shiny wet lips, stretching them wide as he slowly, deliberately spreads his legs. "Nah. I'm good."

Drake slaps him hard across the face, annoyed when that just makes Shane laugh, and shoves his cock back in as he hears Jimmy crow, "Sloppy bitch's already been fucked today," just as he shoves his cock in deep.

Shane just moans, writhing on both cocks, letting himself be yanked forward and back, filled at both ends and obviously loving it. Drake can see his arm working fast, pumping his cock hard, dripping onto the floor, and that pisses him off more. The other guy, whose name he doesn't know at all, sidles around behind Drake. "Try it," Drake dares him quietly, "and I'll break your arms."

The threat does not go unnoticed. The man holds up his hands, retreating to grab a little Waterfae woman, and Drake tunes out the sound of their squealing with the rest of the bar, all his attention focused on fucking Shane's face, making the bitch pay for doing what he did, for being what he is, for letting another man touch him, use him, when that's supposed to be Drake's job.

"Show you," he mutters, even though he can't finish the sentence aloud, can't say *show you you're mine.* He yanks out, working his hand up and down, and he comes with a groan, spilling over Shane's face, messing up his cheeks, his eyelids, his nose, painting those pretty, friction-reddened lips.

It's a good picture, good enough that he can almost ignore the groan he hears as another man floods Shane's ass, giving it a smack when he pulls out. Drake sees another couple of men heading over, and grabs Shane by the chin, yanking his face up. "End it. Now."

Shane sits back on his heels, eyes fluttering closed as he comes over his own fist, letting out a shaky sigh. "Good," he murmurs, licking his lips, moaning as he gets a taste on his tongue. "Fucking good. You taste so good, baby."

"End it!"

He doesn't like seeing the pain on Shane's face. Still, it's better than the emptiness. Shane nods numbly, shakily getting to his feet even as his cock twitches under the effects of the spell, trying to rise again.

When Drake feels how easily it's done, no more than a moment's work and a flick of power, he wants to strangle Shane again. "You could have done that at any time."

"Told you that. Didn't want to. Let's go."

"Where?"

Shane yanks his jeans on, and Drake notices his eyes blaze briefly before the fluids dripping down his thigh disappear. "This place is a fucking bust. Let's hit Jiri up."

"Hell no."

"You got a better idea?"

Drake grimaces at the thought, but nods. "One."

Second Interlude

Twelve Years Earlier

It's not difficult to get a reputation for mayhem in Sunrise City. They've got one, Drake and Shane, by the time they turn twenty-one. That's when they go after Velaria the Enchantress, a self-named idiot who's nonetheless famous for being the most fearsome mage in the country.

He can tell Shane's nervous, can see it in the way he takes too long to put on his gloves, too long to sheathe his sword, to buckle everything into place under his civilian gear, just in case they get stopped by the cops due to Shane's unfortunate inclination to break speed limits. Drake can't say he's much more confident—if it weren't for the size of the bounty on her, he'd be just as happy staying several states away, away from the woman who'd had an entire town doing her bidding, away from the woman legend said was immortal, away from the mage called the most powerful one in America.

There aren't many human mages who voluntarily claim the title, wearing it proudly while still attempting to be part of society. Since the appearance of magic in the world in the last century, it's been more and more acceptable to admit a bit of talent for swaying weather patterns, or having a pretty good idea about what will be for dinner the next day, or being able to grab hot pans without being burned, but that doesn't mean most people *talk* about it. Until a couple years earlier, there'd been no section for "mage" on the IRS forms, and Shane had officially been on unemployment. No matter that things are getting better now, mages remain shrouded in mystery, the way they like it.

As such, Drake and Shane have no idea what they're up against, facing someone who's supposed to be the most powerful mage in the country. They've never faced human mages before for exactly this reason, along with the fact that they just plain don't like the idea of going after members of their own species.

Then again, they've got bills to pay.

They track Velaria to a small house on top of a mountain, something that should really be called a lair with how much effort she's put into the spooky décor. She comes out as if sensing their presence, all carefully styled robes and long flowing tresses, voice a sultry echoing thing. "Inferior mortals, I command you to leave—"

Shane swats her with a bolt of power. It's his usual opening move, intended to throw the target off guard and piss them off, usually goading them into revealing previously unsuspected powers. Drake tenses, sword drawn and in his hands, waiting for the attack.

Velaria falls over, flattened by the bolt, lying in a tangled, groaning heap of limbs.

Shane advances, hands held in front of him, one twitching toward the hilt of his sword. "Cut the crap, lady. Stand up and let's go a few rounds."

When she looks up, eyes shrouded by a fall of dark auburn hair, there's genuine fear in her face. "P-please, I don't know who you are, I swear I haven't done anything to hurt you, whatever I did I'm sorry!"

Drake looks to Shane, then down at the woman. "Jesus, how hard did you hit her?"

"Not at all! That blow wouldn't have felled an Earthsprite."

Velaria's eyes widen further, darting between the two men like ping-pong balls. "Y-you would go up against an Earthsprite? What are you?"

Shane blinks at her, nonplussed. "I'm just a mage, lady. Shit, I thought you were supposed to be the best."

"I *am* the best! I'm the most powerful mage in America!"

Shane looks down at her, silently making his point.

Under the weight of that stare, she crumples. "At least, I was. Listen, kid, I don't know what the hell you are, but you sure as hell aren't human."

The confusion Drake feels is nothing next to what's on Shane's face. "But...but everyone's afraid of mages."

"Obviously. Honestly, boy, how do you think we keep everyone from realizing what we can and can't do?" She flips her hair back. "Now leave me alone, I have some important things to finish."

There's a tiny part of Drake that thinks it's a trick, that she's faking helplessness so they won't be ready for her next strike. That's proved certainly, pathetically wrong when they take her hostage in a matter of seconds, delivering her to their buyer in an hour.

Drake finds Shane in the corner when he comes home that night, burying himself in a bottle of whiskey. "Maybe I'm not human. Maybe I never was. Hell, my parents could have just been waiting to tell me."

Drake's lips close over his, a more effective gag than any they own in a box under the bed. "Whatever this is about, we'll figure it out. We'll get to the bottom of it, together."

Shane's smile is too easy to read. Drake never stops feeling guilty for breaking that promise.

Chapter Five

Shane glares at Drake, sour and unamused as they pull up to the church. "This isn't funny."

"Not making a joke. The Church has plenty of good sources for finding things, and they'll always do me a favor."

"Of course they will. You're the only thing keeping them from being fucking destroyed by creatures of the night." Shane slams the car door shut harder than he'd intended, denting it and not giving a shit. Drake seems to think it's his car, rather than whichever nice one he'd seen close by and unattended.

"You might want to show a little more respect. They've got a lot to deal with, you know? It's not like the old days, when anyone with a stupid idea and a wad of cash could start a religion."

"Don't give me a history lesson, you were never a very good student. The Church gets plenty in donations. They're living just fine in their stone walls."

Drake returns his glare, buttoning up his top button before knocking on the heavy wooden door. Shane doesn't bother to do up his shirt—if anything, he scoots down his jeans an inch or so, just to piss Drake off.

The big heavy door opens, swinging out on its hinges as a young priest, no more than thirty, opens the door. "Drake," he says, smiling at the sight and hurrying over to clasp his hands.

"I'd heard there was evil afoot in the city this evening. I'm glad you're unhurt."

"As I am glad you are safe, Father."

"And you're both really glad that I'm okay, right?" Shane drawls, trying not to throw up in his mouth. God, the idea of Drake on his knees for anything, anyone other than *him* is enough to make him retch.

The priest's eyes narrow at the sight of him. "Ah. Vassal. I didn't see you there."

"Good thing everyone's welcome in the church, isn't it?" Shane asks cheerfully. He moves to enter, but Drake puts out a hand, blocking his way.

"Wait outside."

"The Church is inclusive. I know, I saw the pamphlet."

"Shane, wait outside."

"I can come in if I want."

"No. You're not welcome." Drake's eyes are hard, and his grip on Shane's arm is firm. "Not after last time. Wait out here and I'll be out in a few minutes."

Shane sighs, trying not to look as pleased as he feels. It gives him the shivers, being inside that place, not that it's why he made a scene before. That was just basic fun, really, not anything planned out. "If you say so. Worship extra hard to get the gay off, okay?"

"Damn it—"

"Watch the blasphemy! That's very naughty. Do the priests spank you if you're bad enough?"

Drake stops responding, hurrying inside the Church with the priest only too happy to join him.

Shane sighs in relief, watching the door close just as the presence he'd sensed coalesces behind him, resolving into a figure he knows all too well. Another second and Drake would have seen, and that's guaranteed a bad ending. He turns, smoothly sinking down to one knee, head bowed. "Master."

The freezing wind that sweeps through the street would have

made grown men cry, would have frozen small animals to death in seconds. Shane doesn't blink. All his attention is focused on the tall figure swirling into being, cold incarnate forming itself into the figure of a sharp-featured man. Everything about him shimmers, ice-blue and white and green and dark, frozen red, hair nothing less than a waterfall arrested mid-crash. His eyes flick this way and that before settling on Shane. "Vassal. You are on the hunt."

"Yes, Master." Shane remembers feeling afraid of the Ice King. He remembers feeling a lot of things. Now it's form and politeness more than any fear that keeps him on his knees, keeps his tongue in check.

"You seek the Soul-Thief?"

"Yes, Master."

The Ice King's lips narrow slightly. "You've not hunted anything in nearly two years. Could it be that Roy told you of a certain… bargain?"

"He said I'd get my soul back." Shane had tried lying to the Ice King before. It hadn't ended in his favor. Far better to tell the truth and let the ice chips fall where they may than suffer through a punishment like that again.

"And if I were to tell you that he lied? That I promised only him that sort of reward, and none of the others whose lives I hold?" He reaches into the air, long fingers glistening with tiny lights, even as something inside Shane feels the scrape of a fingernail across it. It's the most real the pain has been in years, and he gasps, clutching at his chest, for all the good that does him.

Tears burn his eyes with their heat, and Shane says quietly, "Master, I would beg you to offer me the same."

"Why should I? You are the most powerful servant I've ever had under my command. Tell me why I should willingly relinquish my most powerful tool."

"Because he's no good to you."

The Ice King's head whips around, features sharpening further, obviously wrestling an ancient urge to strike. "Sister Wife."

"Brother Husband," the woman returns, forming out of the air as the Ice King had, and could not be a more opposite picture. The flame to his frost, she wreathes herself in red-gold-orange-yellow, her skin alive with the heat of an inferno, her hair a living, moving creature. Like the Ice King, she wears no clothing, and her bare feet melt the snow where they touch.

Oh, shit.

Even as dulled as his emotions have become, Shane feels a twinge of apprehension. It doesn't take a genius to know that it's not exactly encouraging for these two to be anywhere near each other, whether they're able to master the ancient urges to violence or not. And given the history the two have as far as Shane knows, he's vastly more willing to put his money on "not."

"Why do you say my Vassal is unworthy? He has bested every Vassal you've thrown at him in nine years."

"Because you kept using him past his date of expiration, Brother Husband." The Fire Queen is at Shane's side in an instant, raking long-nailed fingers through his hair, and it's difficult not to twitch and tremble away from the feeling. "How long do your Vassals usually keep? Two, three years? How long before the ice freezes their hearts, their minds as well as their souls?"

"This is no business of yours, Sister Wife. Leave him be."

As powerful as the Ice King might be, he's certainly not above sounding like a petulant child who doesn't want anyone else to play with his toys, Shane observes, trying not to smirk.

"Yet you've had this one for nigh on a decade. How have you kept him viable?"

"He is resistant. Unusually so."

"More than that," she counters, and kneels in front of Shane, staring into his eyes with an expression that burns. He can feel her in his mind, in his heart, and only the frozen peace of the Ice King's touch keeps her out of his very soul.

"Sorry, Mistress," Shane says quietly, feeling the fire surge inside him. "It's pretty empty in there."

She flinches back, startled. "You still have feelings?"

"Pretty much down to pain and lust these last few years. Unless drunk counts as a feeling." Not for the first time, he wonders what the hell these two are, where they came from, along with the rest of the magic that invaded the world a century ago. Most of it had always been innocent enough, old wives' tales that suddenly weren't bullshit, bedtime stories about monsters that started turning up in the newspapers, word of folklore come to life in Europe and the Far East.

These two, though…

He can see the look on her face when she sees what he's done, sees the wall of magic he's slapped around whatever ragged scraps of feelings he has left, protecting them from the worst of the creeping ice. They're dead and frayed around the edges, but the core survives, blazing hot whenever he needs them—notably, when Drake is nearby.

"You see?" The Ice King demands, putting Shane's soul away with a flick of his wrist, and the fingernail's touch vanishes along with everything else, hardening into ice again. "He's still useful to me. Leave him be."

"But for how long? How many of my creatures has he vanquished in the last few years, my King? For all his power, he has a mortal's weak heart. Will you let him go to ice like the rest of them?"

"He's mine to do with as I choose. He has the price of his soul, given freely of my hand, and with no deceit. Is that not correct, Vassal?"

Shane can't exactly deny it. "Yes, Master. I have what I asked for."

"It pleases me not to give your soul back. You will serve me until you join my Frozen Court."

Fuck this.

Shane's lips curl into the barest hint of a smile. The cold is worse than ever, biting and howling in the wind, and it doesn't feel quite so calming anymore. "Very well, Master. As you wish."

He closes his eyes, and starts to lower his barriers, the inner shields protecting his heart, his mind. Everyone who trades a soul to the Ice King freezes in the end, of course. That's part of the price. Most of the Vassals who work for him want power, want everything the power will bring, can't imagine themselves vulnerable with that sort of leverage.

They're idiots. It isn't power that's kept Shane alive longer than anyone's ever spent in the Ice King's service so far. It's desire, hunger, because he alone traded his soul for something he still has no power to possess.

"Vassal. What are you doing?"

"Joining the Frozen Court, Master. I'm weary of the rankings. Rather get it over with right now." It had seemed like vanity at the time, wanting to keep around whatever soiled remnants of himself had remained, but that's fine. It's over now. Seeing Drake again, working with him again…that had been nice. Fucking him again had been better. It was even funny, the way Drake had obviously missed him.

The ice closes over that thought, and he doesn't really remember humor anymore. Now it's part of the ice, like the rest of him, with regrets and fear and happiness.

"Stop. Vassal, I command you to stop!"

"I've done nothing, Master. I undo none of your work. These are my own creation, and I merely remove them to serve you better." He can hear his voice, toneless, emotionless, flat.

"Stop!" The Ice King reinforces the word with his power, but that has no effect on the lowering of the barriers. The Ice King can't control Shane's magic, after all, and the addition of more of his own just hurries the ice along.

Go on, Shane thinks with the last bit of satisfaction he'll ever feel, regret this. I want you to regret this, because I was a good servant, and I had a few more years in me. Look at me and realize that all I'm going to be is a statue, and it's because you took away my last chance to get him back.

He can feel the ice creeping toward his last memories of

experiencing pleasure, ready to take away the feeling of Drake's strong arms around him, of Drake's kiss, the hard press of Drake's cock against his own. *Shit, I'm gonna miss these.*

Except he won't. Not really. Not any more than he'd missed fear, not any more than he misses humor now. Regret froze a long time ago.

"Brother Husband, if you don't—"

"Fine!" The Ice King's voice rings out like a crystal bell's chime, and Shane slams up his walls again with all the power he can muster, clinging to those last few precious scraps of memory with all the desire he can still summon. Desire, pain, anger, and a bit of pleasure—that's about all he has left now, but it's enough. As long as he has the pain, it's enough to keep him alive.

"Yes, Master?" he asks, waiting pointedly.

The Ice King glares at him, and Shane only stares back, expressionless. He probably would have found this funny, once.

"If you are the one to slay the Soul-Thief, you may have your soul back," the Ice King allows, though he doesn't seem happy about it. "This won't be easy. I'll send everyone after it, and I'll let them know the bounty on *your* head is still active."

Shane nods. "As you wish, Master."

He doesn't need to look to see that the Ice King is gone, in a flurry of whirling ice razors. The Fire Queen is still there, looking at him as though he's a curiosity, an intriguing anomaly. "Not many men have ever stood up to him and lived, Mage."

"No, Mistress." Shane rises, no longer feeling the need to kneel. She's not his Master after all.

"I enjoy watching you, most of the time. I think I'll like it less now that you're no longer funny."

Shane shrugs. It's not as if it matters to him, after all.

"Do you know what they're talking about in that Church right now?"

"Where the Soul-Thief is?"

The Fire Queen waves a hand, and an image resolves in flames in front of him, of the young priest handing Drake a long dagger. "It's not much," he says, as if from far away to Shane's ears, "and it will only work once, but it should be enough for one of the Ice King's Vassals."

"Thank you, Father. We have a few chasing us right now."

The priest grabs Drake's arm, pulling him close. "Don't forget the most dangerous one is the man that travels by your side. Don't make the mistake of assuming he is the man you used to love."

Drake's voice is hard when he says, "I know exactly who he is, Father. And who he isn't. I'll do what needs to be done."

There's pain, aching in Shane's chest, but that's hardly new. He sort of loves the pain. It's almost all he has left, along with the insatiable longing that fills him at the sight of Drake.

The Fire Queen sighs. "I miss when you were fun. Maybe..." She scowls at him, shifting liquid-hot eyes searing into his, and pain shoots through him, ripping and burning into the frozen places, igniting all the parts inside him he'd thought dead, not just dormant.

For the most part, he was right. Ice doesn't just preserve, after all. It kills, thoroughly, and there's no point trying to chafe and warm a black and rotting limb back to life after a night in the snow.

But sometimes...

Sometimes it's possible to catch a limb that's been frozen, and to nurse it gently back to life. Not always, and the Fire Queen isn't gentle, no more able to be anything other than her nature than the Ice King is, and the fire in places that should be frozen hurts more than the ice ever has.

Shane screams, not expecting the pain, collapsing to the ground in a twitching, spasming heap of agony as the Fire Queen straightens up, watching him intently. "I have my own stake in you Shane Conell. Believe me when I say that you do not want to prove useless to *me*, no matter what your arrangement with my brother husband."

She leaves no smoke behind. The hottest fire never does.

Damn the Fire Queen. He'd been done with anger, with thinking life was unfair. It doesn't feel quite right still, tingling and pricking against the inside of his skin, but he hoards it just the same, bringing that safely behind the shield.

Already he can feel the ice advancing again.

The tears freeze against his skin and he brushes them away, sending them flaking to the ground. How embarrassing, to cry like a child, like a needy little girl who can't quite believe that her father will protect her from the monsters under the bed. What an idiot, he'd always thought. Any real monster could just crawl inside her father's head.

Third Interlude

Thirteen Years Earlier

Sometimes, Shane scares himself.

It happens when a sneaky Inferna gets the drop on them, and nearly takes Drake's head off his shoulders with a gout of flame. Shane lashes out with his power, not taking the time to stop and calibrate the strike the way he usually does, his hand moving before Drake even notices the danger.

The explosion blasts a hole in the ground twenty feet wide, leaving nothing but a red-black smear to hint that there'd ever been an Inferna anywhere nearby.

Drake finds him kneeling on the ground, vomiting at the backlash, and gets an arm around him. "Pull it together! There's two more around and we've still got to rescue that boy!"

Shane nods, finding his feet, breaking into a run as he gathers his power for another strike, this time far more controlled. He blasts the Inferna one after the other, this time managing not to level any buildings in the process, and after that it's easy for Drake to defeat whoever's in the building while Shane guards the exit, coming out with a terrified three-year-old boy under his arm.

Drake, mercifully, says nothing.

At least, he says nothing until later. When they're counting money in their apartment, icing burns and paying bills as they snack on supermarket sushi, Drake says casually, "So, you pretty much fucked up a whole city block today. Wanna talk about that?"

"It was aiming at you."

"A lot of things aim at me. It's kind of a consequence of what we do." Drake counts out twelve hundred for rent, setting it in the "out" pile. It's more than what their neighbors pay for the same basic apartment layout, but it's hard enough to find a landlord who'll rent to a mage, let alone one that doesn't have the decency to pretend he's an accountant or something.

"Yeah, well, I don't tend to let them hit you. If you've got a problem with that—"

"You don't usually leave a mess like that." Then, Drake slowly voices what's obviously really on his mind. "I didn't know you could. Not like that. Not just….destroy the whole street like that. I've never seen you do anything in that league before."

"I think…" Shane swallows hard, his heart fluttering a bit in anxiety, even as he counts out the water bill, the electric bill, and helps himself to a California Roll. "I think I'm getting stronger. It happens sometimes, when mages get older. Most stop once they hit adulthood, the way most people stop growing when they're teenagers, but I guess some don't."

"You guess?"

"What do you want from me, Drake? My folks died when I was ten, I wasn't exactly taking master classes. And it's not like there's some big secret Mage Council where we all get together and drink Hawaiian Punch and decide how much tax we should charge on love potions. I mean, okay, there probably is something a bit like that, but I've sure as fuck never been invited."

A strong hand closes around his arm, and the world spins for a second as Drake yanks him sideways to lean against his shoulder, running a hand through his hair. It should be patronizing, but as wound up as he's been all day all Shane feels is relief. He nuzzles into the touch, relaxing at last into the reassuring weight of his boyfriend's broad shoulders. Damned if it doesn't feel like there's nothing on earth that can touch him here.

"I think it happens sometimes," he continues, now a thousand times easier, cradled against Drake's body. "Sometimes you go through a second adolescence, I think. The only other stories I've heard about mages who suddenly got a lot more juice are about idiots who make deals for power, trading away stuff like years of servitude, or even their souls."

He can feel Drake shiver beneath him. "Hey. Let's make a rule right now, okay?" he rumbles. "No deals. No pacts, no treaties, no nothing that'll ever lock us in. Nothing we can't undo. Nothing that binds us to anyone other than each other."

Shane kisses him, deep, soft, the taste always familiar no matter how much things change. "I'd never want to be bound to anyone but you anyway. Yeah, it's a rule."

Chapter Six

"He's dangerous. He's far more dangerous than this creature you're fighting, because you'd never even *think* that something like the Soul-Thief isn't a threat."

"I know Shane is a threat." Drake's weary with the repetition of the words, of how many damn times he's had to insist that yes, he knows the risks, and yes, he still wants to follow this thing as far as he can.

He can't be angry at the priest, though. Father Aaron is only doing his job, trying to protect the Champion.

"He doesn't respect the Church!"

Drake has to actually crack a smile at that, no matter that it's a crude thing to do under the circumstances. "I think I figured that out when he crashed service and told everyone he used to… well, you were there."

It took Drake nearly three years to stop being so angry he wanted to attack Shane whenever he saw him after that, after Shane had staggered into service drunk off his ass and announced that the only thing Drake Young was better at than killing monsters was sucking cock. The accompanying magical illustrations were, as far as Drake was concerned, a bit unnecessary.

"Yet you still travel with him."

"I didn't plan this, Father. The monster has Deborah's soul.

Shane agreed to help me save her before killing the Soul-Thief. He had no reason to, other than to try to buy my goodwill. I…" Drake runs a hand back through his hair, frustrated. "You know how powerful he is, or at least I know you've heard about it."

Father Aaron shifts uncomfortably. "I heard that he once killed a thousand people in an afternoon. And that he was the one responsible for the New York City Forest."

A brief smile flickers across Drake's face. "The forest…okay, I'll give you that one, it was a pretty cool piece of work. It made sense, if you knew what he was actually trying to do. And the other… that was after he turned. I know he's killed a lot of people. He could probably wipe out Sunrise City with enough time to plan and access to resources."

"So can a bomb."

Drake shrugs. "That's kind of what I mean by resources. There's probably not much we could do to stop him if he was really intent on killing everyone. He's good at making his magic work with technology. I've seen him start prank calls on telephones that called every single person who owned a phone in the state and told them the same stupid joke. And that was when we were seventeen. I honestly don't know what he could do now."

"Yet you intend to still work with him?"

"Do I have a choice?" Drake rubs his head, and damn it, this is unfair. He especially hates how little moral high ground he can take when he's been having sex with Shane again, feeling as close as he can to the way it used to, even though he knows what a bad idea it is. "Father, all I want in the world is to have the man I love back. I can't. He's dead. He says he can get his soul back, but he's been saying that for nine years, and it hasn't been true yet. I *know* that the man out there isn't—look, Father, you folks are the ones who offered me the post, if you don't like the fact that I'm gay you can find yourself a new Champion. I don't feel like putting up with a lot of sidelong looks the whole time."

Father Aaron flinches at the sharpness in his tone. "My

apologies. Of course we want you to remain Champion. But this is a sacred space. If you must discuss your homosexuality, please do it elsewhere. Or here," he adds hurriedly, as Drake starts to unfasten the sword from his back. "Here is fine, really. I, ah, forget myself sometimes."

Damned right you do. I'm the only person who's ever lasted more than a year against the things hunting your flock, and you should know better than to piss me off. Drake relaxes, eyes wary. "Okay, then. So stop thinking I'm gonna team up with Shane. I know what he is. There's no risk of me getting emotionally involved."

Father Aaron doesn't look convinced, but he nods nonetheless. "Here, I have something for you."

This part isn't unusual. Sometimes the Church has a habit of collecting pretty fantastic weapons, and frequently manages to get convenient ones into his hands at the time of big oncoming battles. The priest turns, opens a small wooden box, and draws out a long, sharp, thin-bladed dagger. "Our order was given this as a token of gratitude by the Fire Queen herself, many years ago. It's been purified by the mages who work for the Church, off in Europe, and they've deemed it safe for your immortal soul to use. It can unmake ice, as well and efficiently as any flame, but far safer to carry in your pocket."

"And it works on humans?"

The priest's mouth twists. "As well on a normal human as a normal blade. Better on a Frozen creature. At least, that's what our mages say, and you know how unreliable mages can be."

"You haven't tested it out?" Drake asks, pointedly ignoring the comment about mages.

"It's only to be used once. After that, it's no more than a regular knife, if a well-made one. It's not much, but it should be enough for the Ice King's vassals."

"Good," Drake mutters, turning the blade over and over in his hands before sheathing it in his belt. "We've got at least one of those on our tracks."

"I meant you could use it on—"

"I know what you meant, Father. I'm being gracious enough to ignore it. Now, do you have any leads on where the Soul-Thief might be?"

The priest hesitates, but shakes his head. "I'm sorry. All I know is that for a creature of that size to have penetrated so deeply into the city without raising an alarm, it must have a master, someone powerful. I'd suggest looking at the larger gatherings of nonhumans."

Drake nods shortly, thinking privately that a simple "no" would have sufficed. Being unhelpful is one thing, but giving dangerous advice is far another. Just because he's tangled with groups of immortals and survived, or fended off a few attacks, doesn't mean he'd intentionally want to go looking for them.

Not for the first time, he wonders how exactly the Church chooses their Champions, and whether they try and kill them off on purpose, or if they're just that bad at knowing how to do their jobs. It's probably incompetence, he realizes sadly. There's no way malice is that successful. That's simply not the way of the world.

With a sinking feeling of acceptance, Drake makes his way back outside. He has to look around for a second before he sees Shane, lying in a crumpled, twitching heap on the ground, looking for all the world as if he's been tortured.

Drake runs to his side, ignoring the warnings in his mind that Shane can't be trusted, that he's still very dangerous, that he's not the man he used to be. He grabs Shane by the shoulders, shaking him gently and calling, "Shane? Shane? Can you hear me? What happened? God, I was only gone fifteen minutes!"

"Long enough," Shane gasps, and there are actual tears on his face, some hot, some obviously frozen from the cold. "My boss showed up. I'm..." His lip quivers, and his hands come to rest on Drake's strong arms, clutching him close. "I'm not exactly feeling a hundred percent right now. Tell me you at least got something good out of that rat bastard."

Drake winces. "I wish you wouldn't call him that. He's a good man, and you brought that fight on yourself, what with how you came into service a few years ago."

"Spare me, I don't want to hear about your new boyfriend."

"Father Aaron is not—"

"I meant God. Were you cheating on me with him when we were together, baby? Did you wait until I was asleep and get on your knees for him?"

Drake stands, dumping Shane onto the ground in a heap. "Get up," he says coldly, glaring down at him. "We've got a long ways to go, and I don't want to carry your lazy ass the whole way."

"Long ways?" For all the biting sarcasm he's been throwing around, Shane looks unsteady on his feet, as if he could easily collapse at any moment. "Where are we going? Do we have a lead after all?"

"Nope. That's why we're going to see Jiri."

"Yes!"

"You're paying her."

"Damn it!"

Drake finds himself smiling, no matter Father Aaron's warnings echoing in his head. It *is* too easy to think of Shane as the man he used to be, the same way he starts to smell his mother's baked chicken and rice if he craves it hard enough. No matter how Shane might make his old jokes, suck his cock, nuzzle up to him and nip at his earlobe the way he used to, he's still soulless, still a creature of the Ice King with no way to feel. Everything it looks like he's feeling is just a reflex, the twitching limbs of a headless chicken, designed to mess with him and play on *his* emotions.

Yeah, he knows that's the truth. It doesn't make it any easier to ignore when Shane cuddles up to him on the drive, hand splaying over his thigh, tracing gentle patterns.

"Remember that time we ran out of food on the road?" he asks, unable to stop himself because Shane seems the same, if even for a minute.

Shane frowns, white teeth worrying at his bottom lip a bit. "Not sure. Remind me? Doesn't come as easily lately."

"In the Adirondacks. We were tracking a Wielie, and it had made off with some kid."

"Monsters tend to do that," Shane agrees absently, flicking on his wipers as it starts to snow. "I think they take the kids because it freaks us out more, as humans."

So he still thought of himself as human. Good. "We ran out of food on the second day, and you started bitching almost immediately."

"I used to get pretty hungry." His voice is odd, almost curious, as if he's asking a question. It's creepy, and Drake nods quickly, changing the subject.

"You kept trying to summon food, but you've always been so bad at figuring out organic things."

"Never knew much about 'em. Always lived in cities?" The question is strange, as if Shane still isn't sure entirely who he even is. It's the kind of thing that had made Drake leave in the first place, not content with living with a man who only looked like his boyfriend.

"Then you—"

The car hits a bump, and Drake slams into the door. "Damn it, watch the potholes!"

"Wasn't a pothole. It was a dog."

Drake's eyes go wide. "Shane, stop, it might be someone's pet."

"Was someone's pet," Shane says, unconcerned. "I saw a collar. So, we were in the mountains?"

He saw it clearly enough to see the collar, and he didn't bother to swerve. Drake swallows hard, looking out the window, not even sure if he wants to know what's coming. "Never mind," he says at last, and brushes Shane's touch off his thigh. "It was a boring story anyway."

Fourth Interlude

Sixteen Years Earlier

Drake wakes in the middle of the night, and he *wants*.

It's not anything he usually craves, usually more than content to grab his boyfriend and bend him over the arm of the couch, shove him to his knees in the shower, or fuck him on the kitchen table just after breakfast, but God, sometimes that ache is strong.

He tightens his arms around Shane, nuzzling into his neck, nibbling a bit at the skin. That draws a low whine, and Shane swats at him. "Stop it. 'm tryin sleep."

"I'm horny."

Shane buries his face in the pillow. "I'll blow you in the morning, god."

"I don't want your mouth. I want your cock."

Shane stops grumbling. It's a rare enough request that it's still something of a novelty, no matter that they've lived together for a few years now. "Oh yeah? What brought this on?"

"I don't know. Fuck me?"

He's on his back in an instant, Shane kneeling over him to press long, sucking kisses against his neck, arranging them so they're pressed body-to-body, skin-to-skin from chest to feet, sliding slowly against each other. As much as Drake's filled out, Shane has as well, all long lean muscle on a frame that's shot up nearly a foot since he was fifteen.

It's been an easy month for business, something obvious by the lack of any fresh bruises or cuts on either of them, no casts or braces required for basic movement. Either the creatures they catch are getting more and more eager to die, Shane had remarked, or they're getting far, far better at killing them.

Drake closes his eyes, still sleepy no matter that his body burns with Shane's touch on his chest, one thigh sliding up between his legs. "Sometimes I wonder why you stay with me."

"Don't be an idiot. I love you. Hand me the lube."

Drake grabs it from the bedside table, passing it over, and bites his lip when he feels the first press of a cool slick finger against his hole. It wriggles carefully into him, Shane always conscious of the fact that he's not as practiced at this, neither of them as used to the other this way, neither of them quite sure how to make it good.

Still, variety is nice once in a while, and makes up for a lot of awkward fumbling.

Drake lets his thighs part, sighing at the slight ache of two long fingers pressing inside him now, eyes locked on Shane. "Always think you're gonna find a mage and run off with him. Someone who can keep up with you."

"Don't be fucking stupid. There aren't any mages around who can keep up with me." Shane bends to kiss him, sucking on his lip, his tongue, as he slides a third finger inside. "Shh, don't tense up, trust me, I'm not gonna hurt you."

It's true, for all it's strange. Drake wonders sometimes about Shane's family, the mysterious mages he never talks about, the ones who had apparently been so powerful and yet been unable to stop whatever tragedy had befallen them. Then again, he tends to shy away from the subject, knowing how Shane gets whenever it's brought up. Whatever happened, they were apparently powerful, if Shane's any indication. Of all the humans they've gone up against, very few are even a match for *Drake*, and all he's got is a good head on his shoulders, a good gun, and some martial arts training. Against Shane, there's no competition.

He wraps his arms around Shane's neck, pulling him down close as he rocks into the touch, almost, *almost* enough, definitely good, filling that place inside him that only feels empty once every several months. "So you're not gonna get tired of your pet human?"

"Not as long as you keep making such cute noises when I fingerfuck you. Spread your legs, baby, let me in."

It's hard not to feel vulnerable like this, even when he wants it more than anything right now. Hesitantly, he lets his thighs fall apart the rest of the way, eyes trailing down Shane's torso, fixing on his cock, hard and dripping and rubbing insistently against his. "You can take a little revenge, if you want," he gasps, as Shane angles down to rub against his ass, not quite pushing inside yet. "If you wanted to smack me around a little, I wouldn't—"

"That wouldn't be revenge." Shane kisses him again as he pushes in, going as slow as he ever has, giving Drake time to adjust to every slick inch as he's stretched. "I love it when you slap me around, and it gets us both off, so stop talking about revenge. The—shit, you're so fucking tight—only revenge I want is to, to, to make you feel as—"

"Stop talking."

Shane shuts up.

He moves slow, Drake breathing deliberately, trying to focus on the pleasure of that filling ache inside of him. It stings, no matter how careful and slow Shane goes, no matter how much lube he uses, and most of the time Drake has to concede that he's just not built for this, not like Shane obviously is.

Still, sometimes there's nothing he wants more.

He sighs through his teeth, shoving down into each thrust, running his hands down Shane's back to grab that perfect ass, squeezing it in his hands. "Fuck me," he says into Shane's ear, following it with a nip of his teeth. "Fuck me, fuck me, Shane, just—"

Shane loses his control, every bit that he's been holding back in the attempt to be gentle, and slides in to the hilt, making Drake yelp. "Sorry. Sorry, you just feel so good."

"'S fine, keep going!"

Shane gives him a startled little smile, happiness-anxiety-amusement-lust flitting across his face. "God, you really want me bad tonight."

It's way past time to deny anything of the sort, and Drake doesn't try, bucking down into Shane's thrusts, loving the expression on Shane's face when he loses his mind, loving the kisses and the bites he accumulates, loving the way Shane's gentle hands are such a stark contrast to his deep, thorough thrusts.

He feels it when Shane comes inside of him, reaching down to stroke him off until he follows a few seconds later, shaking and twitching and groaning as the ache finally, finally goes away.

"Fuck," he sighs, as Shane gently pulls out to flop onto his chest.

He can feel Shane smile against his chest. "That hold you over for another year?"

"Probably. Thank you."

"You're making me breakfast. Least you can do after waking me up."

Chapter Seven

Madame Jiri's Palm Reading and Tarot hasn't changed since the last time Shane was here. It's still a little dump of a place, tastelessly decorated inside and out. Hell, for all Shane knows, she does it on purpose. The whole Blind Psychic thing is probably some sort of draw for idiots who think spiritual powers are linked to outward appearance.

It's annoying to have to buckle and unbuckle their sword belts every time they get in and out of the car, but it's better than courting accidental impalements, and teleportation is still too inaccurate to be worth the trouble. Besides, Shane hasn't quite mastered the art of showing up with clothes on, though he's so far managed to laugh it off as intentional.

Shane knocks on the bright pink door, sending out a little trail of his power to see if Jiri's inside. It's swatted away after a moment, and a few seconds after that, a familiar old woman opens the door. "Rude," she says without preamble, confusing Drake. "You always were rude, Shane Conell."

"I haven't changed that much."

"And that's a pretty lie. Drake, I wasn't expecting to see you again after last time." Jiri doesn't look like anything other than a short, squat, wrinkly woman. Her eyes are droopy, her skin sallow, and her hair is not only pure white, it's obviously been falling out for some time now, leaving her with patchy clumps where it's abandoned her head.

Then again, no human woman would have been able to parry Shane's magic like that, no matter how "powerful" a mage.

The disguise is a good one, and thorough. Shane's even seen what lurks underneath the false skin, and he can't see more than the faintest trace of it peeking out. A normal human would see even less. He has no idea what Drake sees.

"With all due respect, Ma'am, you poisoned me," Drake points out, but Jiri waves that away.

"A job's a job. You knew the risk when you paid my price. Come in, come in."

The inside is just as revoltingly tacky as Shane remembers. A bright yellow couch with orange slipcovers fills up most of the room, with pastel pink curtains and a mud-brown carpet, not to mention eye-burning knickknacks purchased from every part of the extensive Ethnic section of the local Farmer's Market, something Jiri never seems to get enough of. The whole place reeks of patchouli incense, probably the only thing strong enough to cover up what really happens in here.

Jiri seats her wide, wrinkly self on the most comfortable armchair in the room, navigating with no difficulty despite her obvious blindness. "I've raised my prices," she begins, and Shane doesn't bother sitting on the ugly couch.

"Then we're leaving. You already ask for too much."

She glares at him, and a whip of power catches him across the cheek, sending him sprawling on the couch as Drake tries not to snicker. "Rude again. I'm also raising the value of what I'm selling. Three facts about your subject, not just one. And you get the full package, past, present, and future."

"All definite?"

"You know better. Definite past, probable present, possible future. Take it or leave it."

"And the price?"

The old woman sips a cup of tea that's magically appeared at her elbow. "I'm ready to procreate."

Drake makes little choking sounds behind him, but Shane only shrugs. Maybe a few years ago he would have felt disgust, but this is far and away different from the usual numbness. This is the sort of numbness only acquired by spending a significant amount of time in Frozen Court orgies, where there's no telling what anyone will turn into.

Drake would hate it, he thinks, with a dark little smirk. "Fair enough. Your people go into heat, huh?"

"A rude way of putting it, Mr. Conell. But yes."

"Okay." Shane stands, already plucking at his sword belt. "You mind if I cast an illusion on you? So you don't look so ugly?"

Another whip of power arcs at him, but Shane's ready this time, catching it with his own and sending a shock back down it. Jiri starts in surprise, blind eyes wide, and the power withdraws. "Do that again," Shane says softly, "and it'll be something worse than a shock."

She nods, and he can almost feel the disdain radiating off of her.

"Right. So. Let's get this party—"

"Not you, Ice-Heart. Him."

God, Shane can't help but laugh at the expression on Drake's face. It's as if he's been asked to make out with a Wielie, all severed limbs sewn on wrong and prehensile tongue. "Um… Shane's footing the bill this time, Ma'am. No offense."

Jiri sips her tea. "No deal."

Drake stands, giving her a respectful bow. "Thank you for your time. We'll see ourselves out."

I forgot how damn squeamish *he is about sex sometimes. Well, with anyone but me. Shame, that was our best lead.* Shane opens the door, flipping the old woman off as he goes, and has nearly shut it behind them when he hears what he's been waiting for.

"Wait!"

Slowly, trying not to smirk because she's so obvious, Shane

opens the door. "Yes? Did you reconsider after all?"

Jiri scowls at them, hopping off the chair with the spryness of a woman half—a quarter her age, at least, waddling over and glaring up, up, up. "You are rude, and your heart is ice. He is handsome and kind."

"I'm rude and my heart is ice *and* I'm handsome," Shane counters. "And I'm willing to stick my dick in you, whereas he can't."

"You mean won't."

Drake clears his throat, obviously embarrassed. "No, uh, sorry. He means can't."

She frowns, which makes the wrinkles on her face multiply, almost completely obscuring her theoretically blind eyes. "Your vow to the Church leaves you impotent?"

"N-not exactly."

"He's a homo," Shane supplies, taking too much enjoyment out of it, no matter that enjoyment stings as he feels it, tainted by fire. "Can't get it up for a lady, especially not one that looks like you. So it's me or nothing, Medusa."

Her face puckers as if she's bitten into a lemon, and Shane tries not to gag inside. He tries remembering some of those orgies and the really unfortunate creatures he's entertained as a member of the Ice King's Court, but it doesn't do much good. "Look," he says hastily, trying to compromise, "what if I offered you a deal? You want a kid of Drake's so much, and honestly, neither of us really want to touch you. How about we both jack off into a cup and you squirt it in with a turkey baster?"

"Shane! What the hell!"

"Acceptable." Jiri nods, and there's a hint of finality about it, something almost magically binding. "I'll be in the next room taking my skin off."

"Well," Shane remarks as she waddles away, "if that doesn't get me in the mood, I don't know what will."

As soon as the door shuts, Drake grabs him by the collar slamming him into the wall. "Oh," Shane remarks dryly, wiggling a little in the hold, "you want to do it this way, huh?"

"Dammit, don't just promise for me like that! I don't want to have a child running around!"

Shane blinks at him, nonplussed. "Why not?"

"Because I care what would happen to it!"

"You do? Why?"

There's that look again, like he's done something he never would have years ago. As usual, Shane has no idea what it is. This time, he doesn't even bother trying to figure it out, shrugging and twisting in Drake's hold. "Look, this isn't gonna get any different like this. Just let go of me and we can jack each other off and leave. We'll find the Soul-Thief, you can get your friend back, and I can get my soul back. You want me to be that guy again, right?"

The kind of pain he sees on Drake's face is the kind he usually only sees in the mirror, and something about that feels oddly good. At least he's not the only one suffering. At least he's not the only one who still cares. "More than anything."

"Cool. Get me a cup out of the dish drainer."

"This is all kinds of wrong and unsanitary."

"Stop complaining, that's my job. Do you want to save your friend's life or not?"

Instead of answering, Drake shoves him against the wall, back colliding hard with knick knacks, a clock, probably something horrifically ugly. "Damn it," Shane pants, for all that he spreads his legs, "you forget all your other tricks? Or have you just been thinking about fucking me like this for so long you can't remember how to do anything else?"

Drake's eyes blaze, and he lifts Shane with one hand, yanking him around until he's bent over the sink. It's uncomfortable and cold and demanding, and Shane laughs, nodding approval as Drake strips him from the waist down, leaving him shivering and ready, so ready.

"Not inside," Shane gasps, even as Drake rubs the head of his cock over his hole, growling with how ready he is, and Shane doesn't even try not to think that's funny. "You can never goddamn remember to pull out in time, so not inside. She needs it."

"I don't want her to have my kid."

"Too fucking bad, big man, unless you want your friend's soul to rot. Or me to stay like this." Shane arches his back, amused at the way Drake's hard already for all his protests, rubbing against his ass as if mesmerized, hypnotized. "Sometimes I think you do. Your life is pretty slick now, huh? Don't need me around fucking it up."

Drake's hands grab his thighs, but instead of wrenching them apart as Shane's expecting (and to hell with Jiri, they can always jack off again later), he smashes them together, holding them tight. "Keep 'em like that. And if you have to talk, don't talk so much stupid nonsense."

Shane gasps out a laugh as Drake's cock slides between his thighs. "F-fuck, baby, what—"

Drake nips at his ear, harder than usual, slick cock dragging back and forth, and somehow it almost feels more obscene like this. Shane drops his head, feeling himself harden as he watches the head peek out from between his legs with each thrust, simply making use of him, and damned if there's not something hot about that.

It sort of reminds him of something, but his head is a bit fuzzy, and nothing seems to make sense. Instead of thinking about it, he just ruts back into the touch, arching his hips in a slow, sinuous rhythm. "Fuck, baby, good, gonna make me come so hard, love it when you just fucking *use* me like I'm just here to get you off."

"You *are*," Drake purrs in his ear, and one of his hands lands a hard smack on Shane's ass, making him jump with the force of it. "You can take that, right, you whore? Gets you off, doesn't it?"

With how much his cock jumps, it's impossible to deny, not that he'd want to. Shane shivers, moans, thrusting his ass back, begging with words and with his body for more. "Yeah," he pants, "yeah, yeah, it gets me off, do it again."

"Don't tell me what to do. You're topping from the bottom,

needy slut."

The smacks of his broad hand send sparks of pleasure-pain ricocheting through Shane's body, making his cock so hard he's dripping against the sink, rocking into the cool metal with every brutal thrust of the man behind him, with every crack of flesh on flesh.

"Done this before," Shane grunts, slamming back into every assault, begging and writhing under Drake's strong hands. "We have, haven't we? F-fuck."

There's the slightest break in Drake's rhythm, but he recovers quickly. When he speaks again, the words are biting, savage, and his hand comes down harder, enough that he'll leave bruises instead of just reddening the skin. "You don't remember."

"I don't care," Shane whines, and squeaks when one of Drake's hands comes around his throat, using it as just another handle, just another way to control him, yanking him back, leaving off spanking him to pound harder between his thighs, slick now with his fluids, and Shane's close at the feeling, so close, he can hardly breathe—

Drake pulls away from him, tossing him to the floor as he grabs the cup and finishes, snarling in anger, eyes bright as he pumps his hand over himself. Breath ragged, he passes it off to Shane, turning away to lean on the sink. "Do it."

"I—finish me off, please."

"No. Do it yourself."

He doesn't know what he's done now, or how he managed to piss Drake off so much while taking his cock, but he does as he's told, jacking off into the cup, sort of fascinated by the look of the resulting mixture. Slowly, he gets to his knees, then his feet, careful not to spill the cup. "Did I do something wrong?"

"Just give that to Jiri so we can get our information. I just want to get this over with."

Shane rolls his eyes. "Pissy bitch. Have I ever told you that you suck after sex? You're always good during and then you get all angsty and lame."

"Don't talk to me right now. Just go."

Shane twists his neck, working out some of the kinks before setting off to knock on Jiri's door. "Come in," she calls, and he does, unfazed by the appearance of a squat lizard about five feet tall, lying on its back on the tacky bedsheets. "You have it?"

"As promised." Shane passes over the cup, unworried that she'll take the offering and deny his price. Jiri's always been prompt with her payments.

Nausea aside, he does look away when she fertilizes herself, doing his best not to hear as much as he can't see. There are some things man just isn't meant to know, and he keeps his eyes pretty tightly shut until she says, "There we are. Perfect. Now, which would you like first?"

"Present. Where is the Soul-Thief right now?"

Jiri narrows her eyes, something rather more effective when done by a giant lizard. "You're supposed to ask for past first. There is a ritual involved."

"Then why didn't you just tell me past first?"

"It's a *ritual*, I can't just feed you the answers."

"Fine. Past, please." Vaguely, he wonders if the tacky bedsheets are as flammable as they look.

There's a sense of power gathering around the creature, palpable if nothing Shane's used to manipulating. He thinks, in as much as he can convince his brain to remember the past, that he'd been interested in this sort of thing once, before making his bargain.

When the lizard opens her eyes, they shine, swirling with a million possibilities, certainties, probabilities, ephemera made air and light whirling behind her eyes. "The creature has a master, and the master has many creatures. Many of them have shaped your life. The master of the Soul-Thief is the master of the creature who possessed your father twenty-five years ago and forced him to murder your family."

Shane nods. "Okay. Present next."

Jiri blinks her lizard eyes, but continues. "Right now the creature is probably with his master, in the Frozen Court."

That gets a reaction out of him. "The Ice King, huh?"

"Probably."

"Okay," Shane says, standing and adjusting his sword belt, only asking about the third for the sake of form. "Future please."

"If you rescue the girl, it is possible that the Champion of the Church will marry her next year."

Shane freezes. "How possible?"

"Difficult to say. It's the most probable of possibilities right now."

Shane's lips tighten, and he gives the odd creature a bow. "My thanks for your aid, Madame Jiri. Take care of those eggs."

He leaves the room, giving Drake a little smile as he nods to the door. "Ready to go?"

"Yeah," Drake mutters. He turns to pick up his sword and belt. "Just let me—"

Shane blasts him with enough power to send him through the wall, and reinforces said wall at the same instant. He watches as Drake crumples, pulse steady under his skin, and conjures the most awkward, uncomfortable chains he can think of, looping them between Drake's legs, behind his back, around his neck, before locking them shut. "She's just a friend, huh?" he asks the unconscious man, jerking the chains tighter. "You just don't want to let her get hurt? You're just being the proper little Champion? You still want me?"

He jerks on the chains, watching Drake turn a bit purple before releasing them, hearing him choke and gasp in his sleep, and lays a bit of magic on, sending him into the deepest trance he can muster. "I'm gonna go fix things, baby," he murmurs, running a long finger down Drake's jaw. "I'm gonna get my soul back and you're not going to care about anyone else ever again. I'll apologize then, okay? Otherwise it wouldn't mean anything."

"Sorry about the mess," he calls to Jiri, but he isn't. He steps out of the tacky patchouli-scented house, a destination and murder on his mind.

Fifth Interlude

Nineteen Years Earlier

"Let's get out of here."

It's always on his lips, but usually he keeps it back, knowing how it upsets Drake. After a night like tonight…Shane drives with one hand, the other on Drake's thigh, thumb tracing lazy circles through his jeans. "Just you and me and your cheap-ass car," he says softly, knowing Drake's on the sleepy side of drowsy. "We'll just go. Hit the road and pretend we're eighteen and not have to worry about high school bullshit or curfew or anything."

"What about school?" Drake mumbles, turning to bury his head in Shane's shoulder.

"Fuck school. We could be *anywhere*. We can find an apartment with a welcome mat and a window garden and everything. And we wouldn't have to drive your car out to the woods to have a fuck."

"The woodland creatures can be a bit off-putting."

"I mean it."

Drake kisses his shoulder through the shirt, eyes closed. "I'm sorry your foster family sucks. It's only a couple more years. Hey, turn off the light, we're almost there."

The street is silent when they turn the corner, gliding in near-silence as Shane turns off the engine with long practice, gliding up into the driveway. He adds a bit of magic to give it an extra boost, but as usual, Drake doesn't notice. He unlocks the doors, pulling Drake in for a last kiss before he leaves. "Hey, wanna skip third period tomorrow and hook up in the bathroom?"

"Go to class and I'll meet you at lunch."

"You drive a hard bargain." A smile tugs at Shane's lips as he murmurs, "I love you. See you tomorrow."

He's just scaled the fence, scrambling up a drainpipe and hopping onto a latticed edge to swing into his window, when he hears Drake scream.

He doesn't bother climbing down the whole way, lashing out with his power to carry him over to Drake's doorstep in one flying leap, no matter how the impact reverberates through his body in shock. He throws the door open, yelling, "Drake! Drake, where are you?"

Drake doesn't answer, but neither does he stop screaming, and Shane takes the stairs four-at-a-time up to his room. He can't remember afterwards if he'd flicked the light on or just rammed electricity into it by magic, but it flickers until Shane can see Drake clutching his sister Clara to his chest, shaking her by the shoulders, tears streaming down his face.

The bottom drops out of Shane's stomach.

He staggers out the room into the master bedroom, hoping against hope—but no. Mr. and Mrs. Young lie just as still and motionless as Drake's older sister, their sleep apparently undisturbed through whatever had taken place. Shane tries to catch his breath, grabs the doorknob to steady himself, and then he sees it.

At first it looks like a cloud, a wisp of black smoke hanging lazily over the bed. Shane stares at it, focusing on it with his senses, trying to sense something, anything about what had happened.

The cloud blinks at him.

"Shit."

Shane bolts back into Drake's room, trying unsuccessfully to pry his boyfriend's hands off his sister's body. "Drake, baby, I'm so sorry, but we have to get out of here. We have to go, now."

Drake blinks in confusion at him, obviously not registering the words. "I…Shane…what the…what happened?"

"There's a thing here, it killed your family, you have to get out of here before it gets you too. Just trust me, and we have to go!"

"I'm not going anywhere!"

Something flares, some presence behind him, and Shane swears, turning just in time to put himself between Drake and the thing coming in. "Then stay behind me. And if you get smart, *run*."

That's all he has time for before the thing lunges for him, and he's left to fight the monster with a small nightstand and whatever raw power he can summon. It's powerful, but Drake is counting on him, and whatever the fuck the thing is it's *not* going to take the one good thing in his life.

It dies hard, and Shane's twitching and injured by the end, a sprained ankle and a gash in his shoulder not too high a price to pay. The thing coalesces as it dies, forming into a small, hard-bodied creature that bleeds all over the carpet.

Shane pulls the tattered remains of his t-shirt together, wincing as he moves, wiping sweat-slicked hair back from his face. He doesn't dare look at Drake. "I'm sorry about your family. I…I know how that feels."

"You…what did you just do?"

"Magic." Shane shrugs, trying to look a little less terrified than he is. "I'm a mage. Sorry. It's okay if you—if you don't want to be my boyfriend anymore."

Strong hands grab his shoulders, spinning him around and shoving him into a nearby wall. Copper fire blazes in Drake's eyes. "You just saved my life. You just killed the thing that—why wouldn't I—"

"Some people don't like magic." Shane tries to sound like it's no big deal, because this isn't anything Drake needs to deal with, not now. "Why do you think I got bounced around to so many foster homes?"

"That thing. What is it?"

"I don't know, I'm not trained that well."

"There are a lot of things like that? Things that go around and kill innocent people? I mean…" Drake swallows hard, obviously looking for something, anything to latch onto that isn't his family dead in their beds. "I knew there was magic and stuff, but I never thought there'd be any *here*. That's the kind of thing you hear about in like, big cities. Or in Europe."

Shane gives him a wan little smile. "That's me, defying stereotypes. And yeah, there's plenty of stuff that'll just straight up kill you, that's what happened to my family."

"You never told me that."

The memories come back, of feeling that thing in his house, of seeing his mother screaming as it latched onto his father's head, watching him pick up the gun—just a regular ordinary pistol, nothing special—and put a bullet in his mother's head. Then the girls, all three of them. Then the boys, six of them dead. Then seeing the bullet come at him, some instinct making him twitch to the side, leaving him with the world's worst pain and a bloody scalp but alive. Then, last, his father had turned the gun on himself, and the thing had grown fat and bloated and pleased, fleeing out a window, leaving Shane alone in a house of bodies. "Don't like talking about it. Besides, it was years ago, I was just a kid. Look, come to my house tonight."

"No." Drake lays his sister down, closing her eyes and arranging her into something resembling sleep. "Let's go. You and me and my shitty car. Or better yet, we'll take my parents' car. You—in the car. Will you tell me more about this?"

Drake's not making good decisions right now. Shane knows it, it's obvious, and no matter how much he wants to just say *yes* because it's what he wants, he'd like to at least be a better boyfriend than that. "Baby…your family…maybe today you should—"

"Then I'm going alone. I…" Drake's hands start to shake. "I can't stay here, I can't, I can't."

"Okay, okay. Let's go."

Shane doesn't bother getting anything from the Nelson house. He just helps Drake pack a single suitcase, stuffed with clothes and memories and a few books, and get it into the trunk of his parents' station wagon. He drives, because Drake is shaking too badly to operate any machinery, and pulls over so he can kiss Drake's hair, pull him close and listen when he cries. Later, they hear on the radio that everyone on the entire street was found dead the next morning, and a carbon monoxide leak is given the blame.

Shane doesn't mourn his foster family, glad only that he can stop healing himself in the middle of the night so Drake doesn't ask where the bruises came from. He just worries about Drake, holds him and listens and doesn't object when Drake needs to scream and cry and sometimes punch a wall that first week, though he settles down quickly enough.

At the end of that week, Drake says quietly, "I want to kill them. Every last one of them, every *thing* that attacks innocent people and makes ignorant people scared of magic and gives your kind a bad name and kills children in the night. I want to kill them all."

Shane nestles against his chest, giving him a gentle kiss. "Okay."

Chapter Eight

Drake dreams.

He dreams of meeting Shane, of fighting him, of learning what he'd done and the sick betrayal of it all. He dreams of the first time in his cheap old car, thrusting up between his boyfriend's thighs because neither of them had any idea how two men had sex with each other.

The dreams swirl and evanesce, until they resolve into something a bit more solid, figures standing, talking, laughing.

"Champion."

Drake turns at the voice, and a man stands there. very tall, much taller than Drake, and gorgeously imposing. He smiles, nodding his head. "I thank you for watching over my people."

Oh shit I'm meeting God and I'm naked. "I, uh."

"I'm not God."

"Oh. Good."

"I am the god that my followers created through believing in me, the one they believe you serve. It is I who chose you."

So basically God.

Drake nods, forcing a smile. "Sorry about all the times I've messed up. Where am I?"

"Deeply unconscious. I thought it was necessary for you to meet some people."

"Drake!" The voice is familiar, achingly so, and Drake turns just in time to be bowled over by someone a lot smaller than he remembers, a teenage girl with loose brown curls and a sweet, upturned face.

"Clara?"

His sister buries her head in his chest, and there's no way he can hold her tightly enough, not as hard as he tries. It isn't just her, but his parents, surrounding him, holding him, loving him unconditionally. "I—this isn't real, I—"

"It's all right."

His father's voice, after twenty years, sounds exactly the same. It's enough to bring tears to his eyes, and that's not even fair, he shouldn't be able to cry when he's some kind of incorporeal dream self. "Dad—Mom—Clara—god, I miss you guys so much."

"Oh, sweetheart. We miss you too." His mother smells the same, distinctive perfume and a hint of lemon soap. "We've been longing to talk to you."

"This…what is this place? How can I be talking to you?"

Clara shrugs, brushing his hair back from his face. "You tell us, it's your hallucination."

"Well, yeah, but this can't be heaven. Heaven can't just be a place where dead people hang out, that's ridiculous."

The man he'd first met smiles at him. "Would you prefer rolling hills and harps? I think I've got that one ready at most times. Or possibly the darkness of the vastness of space, and your own molecules as stardust?"

"I don't understand."

"It's *your* Heaven, Drake. At least, it will be when you're ready."

Drake swallows hard. "Am I going to remember this when I wake up?"

"That answer will hardly help you now. There's someone else who wants to speak to you."

Another figure shuffles closer, and Drake's heart clenches. There, with more color in his cheeks, more life in his expression than he's seen in a decade, is Shane, smiling awkwardly. "Hey. I, uh, guess you're pretty angry at me?"

Drake's mouth goes dry, his face white. "You... you're not dead. I just talked to you. You just hit me."

"My body, sure. But most of me's been gone for a while. You know that."

It's one thing to know. It's another to see the soul of his lover up here with the other dead people he's loved, hands in his pockets, tossing the hair out of his face. "Look, I don't have much time," Shane says, and Drake knows all at once that it's true, can feel everything starting to melt away.

"No, I'm not ready!" He clings to his parents. He's only said a single word to them, it can't be time, not yet.

"Drake, promise me something, *please.*" Shane's eyes are intense, confused and angry and urgent and pleading. "If you can't save me, kill me. It hurts so much to be split like this. I can't take another ten years, there's no way, so just kill me, okay?"

"I can't, I could never—"

Shane grabs his hand, kisses the back of his fingers, and he's so warm, so gentle. "Do it, and I'll be waiting for you. If you don't, I'll fucking haunt you, I don't even care what the rules are."

Everything starts to fade, and Drake chokes back a scream that it isn't *fair*, he wants to spend more time with his family, with the real Shane, not just this teasing effervescent snapshot.

"Promise me!"

Drake wakes up.

For a moment, he has no idea where he is, or why he's so uncomfortable. Then he remembers where he is, but damn, it still doesn't make sense. "Um," he calls, voice slurring a little bit, "Jiri? Can you hear me?"

"Oh, yes," Jiri says from behind him, quite close by.

Drake tries to move, but stops quickly when that cuts off his windpipe. Damn it, he taught Shane these knots. He was an awful boy scout. "Um, sorry to impose, Ma'am, but would you mind helping me get out of this?"

She thinks for a moment, running one long claw up the metal chain, making it screech until Drake's ears feel like bleeding. "Hmm. I suppose. But only because I don't like the idea of carrying you out of my house. You're very heavy, you know."

"My apologies. I assure you, I don't eat extra for your inconvenience."

"Leave the comebacks to your partner," she advises. "You stay tight. I'm going to go borrow a bonesaw."

It's a nervewracking few hours before the chains snap, the teeth of the saw grinding entirely too close to his skin in blind hands for Drake to be exactly thrilled with the arrangement. Still, help is help, and he stumbles gratefully to his feet, buckling his sword onto his back. "Thank you. Um, I don't suppose you could tell me what you told Shane?"

"I'm not supposed to. Unless you want to pay my price again?"

Drake folds his arms, forgetting that it's useless to try and intimidate a blind person with his size. "Ma'am, the deal was for three facts in exchange for one man's seed. You got two, so at least tell me where the Soul-Thief is right now."

Jiri glares at him. "Only because I like you, and because I don't like the futures I'm seeing if I don't. You'll want the Frozen Court, young man. I don't suppose you know where that is?"

A sense of foreboding settles over Drake like a thick blanket, dampening his spirits and filling him with unease. "Yeah," he says quietly. "I know where it is."

Chapter Nine

Sometimes, it occurs to Shane to make a list, of all the things he's going to do once he gets his soul back. He's been at the Frozen Court when the idiot hopefuls come in, with an itemized list of everything they're going to ask the Ice King for, certain they won't miss their souls when they're gone. Shane's seen people trade for everything from revenge to a woman's love to a billion tax-free dollars, from a perfect body to magic powers.

Sometimes, if he can work up the emotion, he laughs at them.

Usually, he doesn't bother. Nothing amuses him as much when Drake's not around. Drake brings that out in him, brings out the anger and the hunger and the laughter and the pain most of all.

Damned if some stupid Church bitch is going to take that away from him.

"Sneathen Asghar."

Shane turns left. It's not difficult to find the Frozen Court. They're not exactly hiding. They don't need to, not when the only person who can challenge them in the city—

"So, you're going home."

—is sitting in his passenger seat, for some reason. Shane raises an eyebrow, keeping his eyes on the road as he asks casually, "Did I fucking invite you into my car, Mistress?"

"This isn't your car. You stole it twenty minutes ago."

"Yeah, well, I still didn't invite you."

"Are you going to fight the Ice King?"

The thought hadn't really occurred to Shane. "I'd be fucking stupid to do something like that."

"Or desperate. And we both know you have nothing to lose."

"With all due respect, lady, I don't give a shit what you think, and I have no idea why you're here. How about you talk if you're gonna talk, and get the fuck out if you're not?" He doesn't bother with politeness. There's no ritual, no custom to observe here. Even if there were, the Fire Queen's minions are just as soulless as the Ice King's. She's got to be used to rudeness.

"You know you can't possibly hope to defeat him. No human could."

"Who said I was human? No one else seems sure of that."

"You are unusually powerful for a mortal. Then again, magic is so young. Perhaps soon they will all be as you."

"And what about you, huh?" Shane asks, curiosity temporarily overcoming his apathy—something else she'd burned back into him, apparently. "What the fuck are you?"

"I?" The Fire Queen blinks, a couple sparks flying off her eyelashes. "I am. I wasn't, and then I was, and so was he. Now I am, and so is he."

"Wow. What a boring fucking story. Why are you here?"

"I just said, I—"

"No no, not existentially. In my car. Why are you here?"

"To help you. Or, alternatively, to stop you."

That warrants a pause. Shane drives for a few moments, tires crunching over the falling snow, trying to figure out what she means. "Okay. I'm not really getting this. Do I get the choice?"

When she smiles, he feels the heat like standing too close to the oven, like a sunburn he can feel just starting. "I like watching you, and I have few amusements. Fight my first Vassal. If you win, I'll help you defeat the Soul-Thief and give you leverage on my brother. If you lose, I'll stop you from confronting him."

"I don't understand. Why would you stop me?"

"Because I, too, have made the occasional appointment with Madame Jiri. I know that if you confront my brother husband without my help, you will surely die."

Shane takes a corner too fast on purpose, skidding a bit and correcting with a lazy shove of magic in the opposite direction, getting himself back on all four wheels again. "That's bullshit. I only get maybes and probablies."

"I'm very convincing. She always does her best work when I ask."

"Shit, that's unfair. Next thing you'll tell me you didn't have to jizz in a cup, either."

"Do you only make predictions when you're already certain of the outcome? Are you truly a betting man, Shane Conell?"

The hint of a grin tickles Shane's mouth, and shit, he's glad he's still able to appreciate situations like this. "Sure. What are the odds?"

"Two to one."

"For me?"

"Against you."

Shane snorts. "That's bullshit. I'm better than any human mage that's ever lived."

"Well, then. It's a good thing my first Vassal isn't human."

That changes things a bit, and that's not the only thing. The road changes as he drives, scooting around underneath him as he allows his hands to fall off the wheel. "You must really have a bone to pick, huh? If you're willing to help out a mere mortal."

"Who can be our deadliest enemy but our greatest love? The Ice King is everything to me, as your man is to you."

"Drake isn't my enemy," Shane snaps. "At least, he wouldn't be if your brother hadn't gotten involved."

"He—oh." The Fire Queen's eyebrows raise, and she gives a little shrug. "Never mind."

Just as he's about to ask her what the fuck she means by that, the road explodes, the car hurtling through the air fast enough to stun even Shane's reflexes, landing before it hits the ground, frozen in a whirlpool of ice. The Fire Queen, predictably, is nowhere to be seen.

Groaning at the impact, Shane flexes out with his magic, trying to banish the pain of the crash, trying to see what's got his car, but everything hurts.

Metal screeches, filling the air with the scream of it when the top of the car is peeled off to be discarded into the street. Implacable and unshakable, the Ice King stares down at him, disappointment radiating in chilling waves.

Shane stares up at him, trying to figure out how the fuck to get out of this one, wondering what the Ice King is even doing here, and how he could have hoped to do anything about the Soul Thief when his master was the one holding the reins anyway. "Um. Sorry I can't bow, I'm a little stuck at the—"

The Ice King reaches out and grabs his shoulder, and even the cold Shane lives with every day does nothing to insulate him against that pain. He arches under it, back bowing as far as it's able, and everything goes white-blue.

When his vision clears, it's not much of a surprise to find himself in the Frozen Court. Men and women and *other* litter the place, some long since frozen solid, others lounging apathetically, a few drinking and partying even this late at night. When the Ice King surveys his surroundings, everything stops. Slowly, every eye turns to stare at the pair of them, at Shane clamped into a kneeling position, at the Ice King holding him there.

"My First Vassal thinks well of himself." The Ice King's voice isn't loud, but it carries, and there isn't a person in the Court who doesn't hear. Shane wonders, vaguely, whether the past Vassals can hear it as well, even though some of them haven't moved for a century. "He thinks to go against my wishes, to work with my enemy and destroy my creature. He thinks *very* well of himself."

A lot of the other Vassals are smirking. A couple are young enough to still show eagerness behind the cold dead façade, rubbing their hands together in excitement. God, Shane hates them all. He looks for Astra, but she's nowhere to be seen, not even with hair that stands out as much as hers does. At least that's a mercy.

The Ice King doesn't say anything else. He doesn't need to. The second he releases Shane's shoulder, every creature in the room surrounds Shane, moves to him, eyes alight and hungry.

Shane snarls. There's no *I* There's no way he's come this far, that he's given up so much of himself only to end like *I* He's seen it before, participated in it when it's been someone else. Some of the statues are still littering the Court: there's a man with his legs spread wide, a girl on her hands and knees, a young couple holding hands on their backs.

There's no way that's going to be him.

He turns before the first man gets within arm's reach of him, drawing his sword and striking faster than an eyeblink, leaving the other vassal to scream and twitch on the ground. Before he's completed the turn he gathers as much power as he can, every part of his mind focused on the Ice King, only him, because damned if he's going to go out without taking his greatest enemy with him.

He lets loose, channeling the power down his arm, down his sword, arcing toward the Ice King in a strike that could level half the damned city if he lets it—and he just might—to incinerate the smug frozen bastard where he stands.

At least, that's what was supposed to happen.

The Ice King blinks, and the power evaporates, leaving Shane shaken and off-balance, as if he'd thrown a punch at someone who turned to thin air. A split-second later, a bolt of power like he's never felt slams into him, knocking him flat to the ground, holding him there for long enough for the hands to take hold, tearing off his clothes and forcing him to his knees.

He can't see the Ice King, but he can feel his gaze on him anyway, the way he always does whenever he's in the Frozen Court. The Ice King doesn't need to list his crimes, to itemize insubordination, to tell everyone that this is what you get for working with the

Fire Queen. No one cares. All they want to know, these dead-eyed Vassals of an uncaring creature, is that no one cares how much they hurt him.

Shane tries to strike again, but the Ice King's power weighs heavy on his, draining every surge of power before it can be anything physical, until he'd be unable to kill so much as a flea with all the magic he's got left. He feels that, the draining, just as one set of hands—human, at least—grabs his hips after shucking his pants. "Been wanting to do this for years," an unfamiliar voice grunts in his ear, and the blunt tip of a hard cock nudges at his ass.

Shane twists violently. Not *now*, not his *choice*, he only fucks other people to make Drake angry. But without his power, without anything that makes him dangerous, makes him special, he's just a man. He's strong, but so are the people holding him down, grabbing his hair, forcing his legs apart as the first man's cock shoves inside of him.

Whoever the man is, he's not that big, not as big as Drake, something Shane takes savage pleasure in telling him. The man punches him in the kidney before grabbing his hips and rutting in harder, and even if he's not that big, it still aches, he's still not ready.

There's a woman's hand on his cock, stroking him to hardness, and damned if he wants to like being raped on the floor. He feels the tears making their way down his cheeks, and he lets them freeze. Maybe it's easier, in the end, to feel nothing after all.

Something nudges at his mouth, and he blinks away the frozen tears, looking up at—"Roy!"

His second grins down at him, shifting his form to one of the largest men Shane's ever seen, a ruddy-faced man who looks like he should be crewing a Viking ship somewhere. "Hey, boss. Open your fucking mouth."

"Bastard, I'll kill you for—"

That's all he has time to say before Roy slides in the head of his cock, holding his mouth open with a strong hand as he slides all the way in, cutting off Shane's air.

"Aw, quit struggling. We both know you've sucked more cock than anyone in this room. Do you even have a gag reflex?"

He doesn't, not really. That doesn't mean that much cock down his throat doesn't make him choke and cry and struggle for air.

Feeling nothing has to be better than feeling this.

He can feel the ice waiting, always inside him, creeping over his feelings. The magic he's been controlling it with is gone, nothing left to protect him against the ice.

If only pain would go first, but it won't. Pain will go last. He's known that forever.

"Lift him up. I've been wanting that ass for years."

Someone slaps his ass, hard, and he wants to sneer at them, tell them he gets more pain recreationally from Drake than they could ever give him. They flip him over so he's on his back, slamming him down onto some sort of ice table a mage conjures. It's so much easier for Roy to slide down his throat this way, and his legs are yanked wide apart, all the better to let whoever it is fuck up into his ass.

Something warm straddles him, a woman, he thinks, from the general contours he can feel against his torso. He can't see anything but upside-down hairy legs and balls, can't move, can't breathe. He hears a woman purr, "You're not so gay now, are you, boss?" before a tight wet sheathe sinks down around his cock.

"Holy shit," Roy crows, "I think he just gagged for the first time!"

"Oh, fuck you, Roy."

Roy changes while he's fucking Shane's mouth, though the only way he can tell is by the shape and size of the cock lodged down his throat. Sometimes the color of the legs changes, too, from white and hairy to sleek smooth black to stocky and tan. It's an odd sensation, and the cock in his mouth is always too-big, always hard and leaking the same bitter flavor.

Maybe if he just stopped fighting the ice…

"Move over. I want in too."

It sounds like one of the new guys, someone who only let the

Ice King into his life a week or so ago, someone who probably still thinks he made a great decision. There's a moment of awkward maneuvering, and Shane tenses hard, feeling two men standing between his legs.

No—too much, I can't—don't—

New Guy shoves in hard, and Shane gags, choking and drooling around Roy's changing cock as he's spread, stretched too wide and opened by two cocks even as the woman rides him, even as others grab his hands and hump against them. Something hot and wet hits his chest, and even over the pounding of blood in his ears he can hear laughter.

He can feel the Ice King's eyes on him.

After what feels like an eternity, Roy pulls out of his mouth, leaving him to cough and retch and heave breaths while he can. Seconds later, he flinches as Roy comes on his face, hot liquid dripping down his lips and cheeks, up his nose in the awkward position. "There," his old subordinate says with a grin. "Now you look pretty."

Shane doesn't have time to say anything before someone takes Roy's place, and this man's cock is odd, too hard, too smooth, and there's too much hair rubbing against his face. Not a human, then. The taste is strange, if not necessarily worse, and at least his aching jaw has a bit of a rest around the man's slender cock.

At least, he wants something of a rest. The man, creature, whatever he is, thrusts hard and fast and deliberate, using his mouth brutally, and everywhere he slams against the delicate flesh it hurts.

It doesn't sting as much as one of the men coming in his ass, pulling out with a laugh and a slap to his ass, and Shane doesn't even have time to sigh in relief that the nauseating, cramping ache of being so overstuffed is finally gone before someone else shoves in.

The ice creeps over a lot of things. It freezes steadily closer to his core, and he really wishes he could remember what his first time with Drake was like. It was better than this, for sure. If it was with Drake, it was definitely good. He thinks he sort of remembers giving a blowjob for the first time, but that was to an awful foster parent, not to Drake. He doesn't really remember that man's name.

He doesn't remember if he ever told Drake about that.

When the next two men come in his ass, they leave him empty for a moment, laughing at the way he whimpers and twitches. A whisper goes up, and if he weren't having his face fucked by a series of increasingly ruthless men, he might have been able to make something out.

As it is, it's a surprise when something slippery and long winds its way up one of his legs, then the other, each cold slick appendage forcing his legs wide apart. The woman riding him comes, sliding off his dick as she crows, "I've got to watch this."

If everything is ice, he doesn't have to feel what comes next.

He knows what it is. Everyone's seen the creatures that live in the icy pools, inky black and slithering, that only come out whenever there's prey that won't run away anymore. Shane can't stop himself from trembling, no matter how hard he resolves that he's going to become one of the Frozen Court, that he's not going to let himself care anymore.

He's seen it before.

It was funny, then. He distinctly remembers being amused by watching a person thrash around while icy black tentacles wormed their way inside his or her body being slowly filled beyond capacity.

Someone comes in his mouth, and he's free for just long enough to mutter, "Please, don't, Master—"

It's not as bad as he'd expected, at first. One cool slick tentacle slides into him, not much thicker than a man's cock but long, god, it feels endless. Someone starts to grab his face, but Roy grabs the man's arm, pulling him back. "Leave it free. We all want to watch him scream."

Of course they pay attention to Roy now. That talentless hack will be First Vassal now, the best of the pathetic lot now that Shane's going to be decorating the Frozen Court.

He's seen men last for six, seven days as the Court's playthings. At the time, he'd been impressed. Now, he just wonders why they'd bothered.

Another tentacle forces its way into his ass, and this one makes him cringe, arching back and away, trying to escape the cramping ache in his abdomen. He pants, shallow breaths coming fast, and he tries to stay calm, tries to just hold still and let the ice take him and god *damn* it, after nine years of trying to get in the ice is picking now to be slow.

When the third one goes in, Shane starts screaming. He's never been so full in his life, and the creature only holds him tighter with every thrash of his body. It gets tired eventually, Shane knows. He's seen it play with its victims for hours, but it always crawls back to the pool eventually. Then the other members of the Court get nasty.

The ice closes over sadness, and humor, and longing. That changes everything. He can feel the pain, feel it in the most all-encompassing way he can imagine, but he doesn't care if it stops anymore. He doesn't want. There's nothing to want. He remembers Drake, dully, remembers that there was a man with a sword and a really nice ass, but that's fading too, bound away in the ice, and he knows better than anyone that whatever's truly frozen doesn't thaw. It doesn't *ever* thaw.

He still twitches when the creature pulls out of him, scuttling away and leaving his body trembling in agony. His eyes flick upward when the Ice King stands over him, something glowing white-hot and intense in his hands. "I have never cared how much my betrayers suffer," the Ice King says, "only that they do. You are different. You conspired with my most hated enemy to defeat me, and for that, I will watch you know true pain."

Three things happen very fast.

Shane freezes to ice.

The Ice King drops his soul.

Drake breaks down the door.

Sixth Interlude

Twenty Years Earlier

"There's a boy in the street."

Drake doesn't look up, bent over his homework, trying to figure out *how* to get to the answer in the back of the book. "Oh yeah? New boy from next door?"

"I didn't hear they were getting another foster kid, but he must be." Clara strains her neck, resting her fingers against the window, breath fogging up the glass. "Oh, you should give him one of your coats, he looks cold."

"Uh, yeah, I think I have an extra one that Nana gave me for Christmas. He's not fat, is he?"

"No, he's really hot."

Clara snorts as Drake finally looks up from his homework at that, elbowing him in the side when he joins her at the window. "You're so gay."

"Shut up."

"It's okay, Mom and Dad aren't home."

Drake hardly hears her. The boy is short for his age, slender but muscled, like an athlete, probably not far from Drake's fifteen years. He's pale, and pretty, with slightly pink lips and thick glossy black hair, sharp features that manage to avoid pointiness, and legs that are too long for his jeans. There's an inch or two of ankle sticking

99

out, though the primary cause of his shivering is probably from the light t-shirt he's wearing.

"Yeah," Drake says slowly, mouth dry. "Yeah, I'll just…go get that coat."

"Gay!"

"Shut *up!*"

It's the work of seconds to grab the coat, a puffy blue thing that keeps him plenty warm, but is just unpardonably ugly. He grabs a pair of jeans while he's in his room, pauses, then grabs a couple books as well, running down to make sure the boy doesn't retreat back into his house. Just before leaving, he straightens his hair in the hall mirror, trying to look nonchalant as Clara snickers at him. Then, he strolls outside, trying to look for all the world as if he'd just accidentally happened to wander outside with extra clothes and books in his hands. "Oh, hey," he says, affecting surprise. "You're, uh, must be—there's some people—my grandma gives me—"

The sentence goes quickly to hell, and no matter how he struggles, he can't seem to wrestle it back on track. Dismayed, he falters to a stop, unable to quite think of words when he sees the boy's eyes, a deep, sparkling, long-lashed blue.

They're expressive, somehow softening the words as the boy says, "Did you come out here just to stare at the new kid, or are we supposed to be having a conversation?"

Drake's face burns, and he holds out the coat, an awkward peace offering. "My grandma gave me this for Christmas and I already have one I like more, and you look really cold, so I'd be really happy if you took this one off my hands. Oh, and these jeans, I figure it must be a pain finding jeans that fit on a budget, and I have these left over—oh, and I know the Nelsons don't believe in TV, so you might be bored, and I brought you some books. So, here." He shoves the bundle in the new boy's hand. "And my name is Drake. Welcome to the neighborhood."

The boy stares at him, emotions flickering across his face. There's gratitude in the softening of the hard set of his jaw, hurt pride in the way he draws back, relief in the widening of his eyes.

Watching his face probably shouldn't be so captivating.

"I...oh." The boy swallows hard, looking down. "I'm not a beggar or anything."

"No, whenever we have anything left over, we usually bring it over to the Nelson place. I figured you had to be one of theirs because—"

"Because I look like a foster kid?"

Drake can tell that the boy's on the verge of throwing the clothes and books to the ground and storming off, and holds up his hands, pleading. "Not like that! I just—I know everyone else on the block!"

God, Clara was probably laughing herself sick.

"Oh." The boy hefts the clothes up, frowning. "Okay. Sorry. Thanks. Is this a loan?"

"No, you can keep it." Drake shrugs, and damn, this was easier with the ugly girl who'd taken his old textbooks. At least then he hadn't been continually distracted by the fluttering of her eyelashes, or the way her slender fingers gripped the present.

"Shane." The boy juggles the clothes around, offering a handshake, which Drake takes gratefully. The boy's hand is warm, startlingly so, and he doesn't squeeze too hard to try and show toughness. He holds the shake for a little too long before letting go, holding Drake's gaze the whole time.

Drake swallows hard. The last thing he needs is for the kid to think Drake is hitting on him or something. He seems nice enough so far, but he really doesn't need word of a fight like that getting to his parents again. "So, I'll see you around. And probably at school."

"Yeah, sounds good. Thanks."

"It's no problem. I hope you enjoy them." Stupid thing to say. Stupid, stupid, stupid. Drake shoves his hands into his pockets, awkwardly turning to go back inside.

"See you around," Shane calls. "Oh, and if you want to make

out, I'm gay too."

Drake's pretty sure his heart stops for a second, and that he can hear a little shriek from inside his house. All the blood drains from his face, and he stammers, "What? I—I never said…"

Shane shrugs. "Or not. Must've read you wrong. See you around."

"Wait!" Drake hurries after the boy, grabbing him by the shoulder before he can retreat into the Nelson house. "You can't just say something like that to someone!"

"Why not? You gonna hit me?" There's a definite glint of challenge in those bright blue eyes, even as Drake backpedals.

"No, of course not, I just—"

"Then I'll say whatever I want."

"Just because I won't doesn't mean someone won't hit you if you say you'll make out with them!"

Shane grins, and it lights up the whole street. "I know. Pretty good test to see who's a homophobe, though, huh?"

Later, Drake learns that he's not the only person Shane introduces himself to this way, and he's had no shortage of fights over it. But that's after he learns that Shane isn't a mind reader, and that Shane's just as surprised to find out his guess wasn't bullshit when Drake takes him up on the offer behind the bleachers at lunchtime.

It's hard to tell, looking at the excitement, the gratitude in Shane's eyes, why Drake feels like he's the one that's been saved.

Chapter Ten

Finding the Frozen Court isn't a problem. It never has been.

The problem is the sense of foreboding Drake can't shake, the one that comes from the same place as his sword, as the inhuman strength his position as Champion gives him.

He remembers believing in God. Back then, he'd thought of God as a big guy in the sky, granting the prayers of good people and sending sinners to Hell, like a cosmic Santa Claus. He remembers going to church with his family, putting on his best Sunday clothes and loading up the station wagon and trying to mess Clara's hair up without getting smacked.

He'd never made a conscious decision to stop believing in God. It wasn't until the Church had come to him, after he'd lost Shane, that he'd realized he hadn't prayed since the death of his family.

After accepting his post as Champion, doing battle with the Church's enemies, being lent the power to fight the creatures and people that terrorized its members, he'd started feeling the, well, *feelings*. Sometimes they're strong, sometimes weak, and they always feel like danger.

He's never had one as strong as this.

Part of him misses the solid weight of a gun at his hip, back before he'd had the sword. Then again, a broadsword is a hell of a lot easier to explain in the backseat of his car whenever the cops pull him over. There's also the fact that it's a lot more difficult to hurt people by accident. There haven't been many accidents, but there have been some, and more close calls.

Some dark part of him, something practical and analytical, tells him it's stupid to go. There's no point, after all. Shane isn't Shane, and Deborah's probably long dead. He's avoided the Frozen Court for years, because damn it all, he knows how much the Ice King, the Fire Queen, the Darkfae Premier and the Woodsprite Governor want to get their hands on him while he's vulnerable. At first, it had just been because he'd put so many of their people away. Now, he's valuable.

Drake turns the corner, jacket buttoned up against the wind, and the pink-haired girl, Astra, stands in front of his path. "Hey. You should like, turn around and go the other way."

"And if I'm going *this* way?"

The girl spits out a wad of gum into the snow. "Then I'm gonna fight you."

"Come on, girl." Drake unsheathes his broadsword, raising an eyebrow. "I go toe to toe with Shane."

"And he doesn't wanna beat up your ugly face because he likes your butt too much. Come on, Sasquatch. Let's party."

Human mages are weak. They're weak, and they rely entirely on magic, Drake's found more often than not. It's easy to play into her hands, to make a show of ducking bolt after bolt of power, no matter how they'd just fizzle out against his chest if they connected. It's easy to feign berserk fury and swing wide at her with his sword.

"Aw, that's the best you got? Come on, I want to dance!"

She leaves herself wide open, and Drake has to work not to sigh. He fakes a stumble, comes up with a handful of snow that he lobs into her face, throwing her off balance, and whacks her with the flat of his blade.

She tumbles to the ground with an indignant squeak. "Hey! You—"

Drake grabs her hair, yanking her head back. "You," he informs her, "remind me of every obnoxious videogame character I wanted to beat up as a child. Let's see if you've still got the stink of human on you."

"If I what? What else would I be?"

"I don't make the rules." Carefully, Drake turns his blade, nicking the skin of one exposed thigh. The flesh parts easily, but doesn't bleed, and molds back together as soon as he removes the sword. "Lucky for you. Do yourself a favor and freeze over soon, or next time I come after you, you'll bleed."

The girl looks scared. That's good. "What if I bleed?"

"Then I kill you."

"What? You can't! You fucking psycho!"

"Don't look so freaked out," Drake says, sheathing the sword on his back. "Really, you're already dead."

Like a chicken with its head cut off.

He fights a couple more Vassals on his way. They bleed. He cleans his sword off carefully before putting it away, just as he reaches the door to what's ostensibly a large bureaucratic building housing fat old men making obscene amounts of money off of suggesting laws about taxes and tollbooths.

The foreboding is strong, filling his body, almost dragging physically on his hand as he reaches for the doorknob. By the time his fingers brush against it, his teeth are gritted against the pull, trying to force his hand to work in spite of the force pulling against it.

"The hell with this," he grunts, and pulls his hand back, lashing out at the door with the most powerful kick he's ever dealt in years of teaching martial arts. Brittle and cold, the hinges snap, the door slamming to the floor with a boom.

Drake isn't quite ready for what he sees.

He's known for nine years that someday, the man he'd been in love with for most of twenty years would turn to ice. He's known that the easy laugh and long-lashed eyes would freeze over, that there would be nothing left of Shane's jokes and kisses but a statue.

He hadn't expected to have to *see* it.

Shane is on his back, legs spread wide, completely naked, mouth contorted into a scream. Every part of him Drake can see is white-blue and still, smooth and glassy as the rest of the statues in the Frozen Court. There are Vassals all around, the Ice King himself standing by the figure, and in the background Drake can see several dark shapes, any of which could be the Soul-Thief.

Right now, none of that really matters.

He can hear himself screaming as he runs, sword clutched in his hands, and the smart ones run. He cuts down a Vassal too scared to move, another that bleeds most satisfyingly, a young man who fails to prepare a magic strike in time to do any good. A few of them don't bleed, springing back in shock from the blows, unharmed by the magic sword. Most bleed. The Frozen Court isn't a place where much of humanity lingers.

Drake doesn't care. If he'd had a gun, he'd have killed the ones who bleed and the ones who don't, and never thought twice about it. All he can see, no matter where he looks, is Shane's frozen body.

The closer he gets to the Ice King, the more vassals throw them-selves in front of him, hurling spell after spell, throwing daggers and icicles and even a grenade or two. Drake knows better than to let them hit, knows all about the way a vassal's weapon turns the whole man to ice with a single graze, and he's never moved this fast on his feet.

The Ice King, damn him, just watches, eyes cold and unamused, arms folded across his chest.

There's a thing coming at him on several legs out of the corner of his eye—damn it, someone always turns into a fucking centaur—and Drake leaps out of the way, flying back into the wall as the centaur lunges with a spear in one hand, a short sword in the other.

Drake shoves off the wall with one foot, going into a twist that brings his sword crashing down one-handed into the centaur's rump, spraying blood everywhere as it morphs back into a young man, clutching his backside and screaming.

Drake leaves him there to heal himself with ice. He's got more important things on his mind.

The red haze only clears from his eyes when the Court is silent, but for his own labored breathing and the pathetic groans of the people he's defeated without killing. No one stands between him and the Ice King, still standing unworried and almost bored. "You," the Ice King says, surveying his Court, "are not endearing yourself to me, Champion."

"I'm not terribly fond of you either."

"Yet until today you were intelligent enough to stay away from this place. Why has that changed?" The Ice King's smile isn't kind, showing pointed ice chips of teeth. "I've certainly tried enough times to lure you here."

"I remember." That had been years earlier, just after he'd taken up the Church's offer. All of a sudden he'd been sent message after message, telling him that Shane was in trouble, that he had to go to the Frozen Court immediately if he ever wanted to see him alive again.

"I was impressed that you never came. He traded his soul for your life. It takes a special kind of man to have no gratitude for such a thing."

Drake doesn't look over at Shane's body, twisted and contorted in a rictus of pain that will never fade. "I never wanted him to make that deal. I never wanted this for him."

"Would you do the same?" The Ice King's smile curves larger, his toes flexing against the floor. "I'll offer it to you, Champion. His life for your soul."

"No deal."

"He's still alive. I could save—"

Drake swings at him, powerful arms slicing through the air as he brings his sword down with all the force he can muster. There's a resistance, a force opposing him, but there's the power granted to him as well, the one that makes him more than just a man, and he bears down with every fiber he can, physical and mental. The blade turns, and he misses cleaving through the Ice King's neck, but a chip of ice hits the ground, knocked from the King's shoulder.

Everything goes silent.

The white-cold fury of the Ice King surges through the hall in a heartbeat, a soundless cry that sets every nerve Drake has on edge, and the Soul-Thief crawls out of the shadows, whole and healthy with all six legs intact. Next to it, another, and another, and another of the same emerge from the shadows, scuttling out to surround the two of them.

There's no escape. There's no hope. Drake will die here, he knows, and all he can hope is that it'll be a clean death instead of being rent to pieces and corroded beyond recognition by the acid of the Soul-Thieves.

His next thought is a bitter one, something he hasn't felt since he was an angry teenager railing against the unfairness of life, picking up a shotgun for the first time.

At least no one will miss me.

Hell, maybe some people are even waiting.

That's no reason not to go down without a fight. Drake reverses his grip on the sword, transferring it to one hand as he leaps, the other going to the dagger Father Aaron gave him at the Church what seems like forever ago. He strikes up with the sword, and the Ice King catches the blow on his hand, wrenching savagely enough to twist Drake's arm out of its socket, something that hurts a lot worse when the Ice King knocks the sword from his hand.

The power that's surged through him since the previous evening, when he'd strapped the sword to his back, vanishes. Drake is left shaken and in pain, trying not to black out from the sudden aches and injuries coursing through his nervous system, subsumed until now by the power granted to him as Champion.

That's one of the prices of being Champion, after all. Unless he holds the sword, he's no more than a regular man. He tries to bring up the dagger, but his arm is heavy, unresponsive. The cold is agonizing, shockingly painful without his protection, and Drake can barely breathe, blinking back tears.

"Little fool who thinks himself large. This is your final chance to make a bargain with me."

Drake falls to one knee, struggling to keep his eyes open. "Yeah, I'd rather not. Just don't put me in an embarrassing position, okay?"

The Ice King's smile flashes and in his hand a long, slender sword materializes. "As you wish, Champion."

Before the sword can come down, ice shatters behind Drake, sending chips everywhere as a tortured scream echoes through the Court, startling the Ice King enough that he pauses. His eyes narrow, even as Drake resolves not to turn around, just in case it's a trick.

Except.

Except he knows that voice, even if he's never heard it scream like that before. The adrenaline from just the possibility gives him the energy to throw himself to the side, the Ice King's sword missing him by a millimeter. He can feel the wind from it, the icy chill permeating through him, but everything's damn cold in this place. If something wants to hurt at this point, it needs to get the fuck in line.

The Ice King snarls, brings the sword up again while he lashes out with power with his other hand, keeping Drake stationary on the floor with just the force of his mind. He tries to move, tries to even twitch, but he's held, pinioned, as the sword comes down for one final blow.

It doesn't hit him.

Something warm and solid hits him instead, knocking him away from the blade, sheltering him, and Drake's mouth goes dry as Shane lifts his head. "Hey," he says wearily, eyes flickering between amusement, surprise, joy, and pain.

Drake can't speak. He can't even blink around the shock of seeing Shane alive, seeing him be *Shane* again. The only thing that makes sense is that he's died as well, but damn, if he has, Heaven is a lot more painful than he'd been hoping.

Shane appears to be suffering from no such injuries. He's still stark naked, but he grabs the dagger from Drake's hand, flipping it once before grinning, going into a somersault so fast he blurs in front of Drake's eyes.

He comes up and leaps, all long limbs and grace, bounding off the nearest wall to build up speed as he runs around behind the Ice King, dagger outstretched.

As fast as Shane is, the Ice King is just a shade faster. He turns, his own blade whipping up so fast Drake's sure he'll hear a sonic boom in a second, and the deadly sword draws a trail of blood down Shane's arm.

Drake cries out, knowing what follows, watching the scratch turn ice-blue and spread as Shane lands in a tumble, coming up to clutch at his arm. Something flares in his eyes, and he snarls, "This is your own fault, *Master*! You never thought it was important that I was so damned resistant to you? Maybe now you'll see why!" He wipes at the blood, and the ice falls away to the floor, leaving pink healthy skin beneath.

The Ice King stares. It slows him down, the surprise, and when Shane comes at him in a whirling fury of magic, some of his strikes hit. "Here," he yells, "catch this!"

He tosses the dagger, missing the Ice King by less than an inch, and it buries itself in the wall behind him.

The Ice King laughs. "That little dagger is the best you can do, Child of Flame? Why waste your last move on such a throw?"

Shane grins. "I wasn't throwing it at you."

Drake wrenches the dagger from the wall with his good arm, putting the absolute last of his energy into one last thrust.

The blade sinks into the Ice King's back, and Drake screams with the force of the backlash. Ice travels up his arm, threatening to turn him to ice, to blast him out of existence, as if he's at the epicenter of a howling blizzard full of daggers.

"Hold on!" Shane shouts over the wind, and Drake tries, he

does, even as the Ice King thrashes on the blade. He can hardly do anything else, not when his hand feels frozen solid on the hilt.

Shane tackles him, wrenching him free of the writhing mass of destructive energy, and the next second the cold vanishes, the whirling ice rebounding off a clear dome of light surrounding the two of them on the floor.

"Neat trick," Drake gasps, trying to flex the pins and needles out of his hand. "That something you learned recently?"

Shane laughs, warm and genuine and so, so real. "You have no idea how much I've learned."

His kiss is as familiar as it is welcome, soft and hungry, nipping at Drake's lips, and it's shocking how it can taste the same as it has for the last nine years and yet wholly, completely different. It doesn't matter that the world is destroying itself around them, that the floor is ripping up in great chunks of ice and statues are shattering, ice chips whirling up in a massive tornado. None of it matters but the touch of Shane, the real Shane under Drake's hands, against his lips, pressing up between his legs.

He tastes salt, and it's impossible to tell which one of them is crying until Shane pulls away, wiping his eyes on the back of his hand. "Sorry. God, I can't stop."

"It's okay." That's not the word for what it is, but Drake can't really think of a better way to say it. "You're kind of behind on feelings. I don't mind if you play a little catch-up."

He expects Shane to wipe his face and put on a fake smile. He's never really known how transparent he is when he's upset, always thought he was better than he was at hiding his feelings. Instead of laughing it off, Shane sort of collapses, burying his head in Drake's chest and shaking with silent sobs, tears landing hot on his shirt.

Drake tries to put his arms around him, but what with the one that's still trying to turn to ice and the other that's dislocated, he doesn't manage much more than ineffective flopping.

That seems to snap Shane out of it, dragging a hand back through his hair to get it out of his face. "Sorry," he mutters, sniffing as he reaches down for Drake's icy hand. "Sort of lost control there. Forgot how good it felt. Here, try to flex?"

The roof falls down, bouncing harmlessly off the shield as Shane chafes his hand slowly between his own. The feeling returns painfully, less pins and needles and more swords and daggers, but it does return, which is an immense relief. It's only a few minutes before Shane's letting go of his hand, turning to the shoulder. "Not as great with this. I can only pop it back in, I can't make it stop hurting."

He doesn't give any more warning than that before grabbing Drake's arm, using his own considerable strength to lever it properly into position with a swift, agonizing jerk.

The throbbing uselessness fades, replaced by a much more bearable pain. Then Shane collapses down to his chest, burrowing and nuzzling as Drake's arms come back around him. The rest of the building finishes falling, leaving them in the dark, the strange otherworldly chill finally gone.

It's quiet, in the settling dust, kept out by Shane's barrier. It's too dark to see much of anything, but after a moment, Shane carefully lowers the barrier. "Everything sort of fell around us. Well, on top of us, but it looks pretty stable now."

"How can you see?"

"Okay, it *feels* pretty stable. You know, for the wreckage of a fallen building."

"Can't be that hard to bust our way out, can it?" Drake asks, experimentally prodding at a slab of wall propped at a 45 degree angle. It doesn't move any more than it did before it fell, as solid as anything.

"Nah. But I was sort of thinking…" Shane's hands are hot on Drake's shoulders, gently guiding him onto his back. "We're tired, right? And we're safe, and we're stuck, and my magic's gonna take forever to recharge after a fight like that, and—"

"And?"

Shane's mouth swipes against his neck, wet and warm. "And

I've missed you for nine years."

Drake tries to remember composure, that he has a million questions, but being with Shane is a million times more distracting than being with the thing that had been Shane, and he wasn't even great at resisting that. "What do you remember?"

"Some. Parts. Mostly everything that happened in the Frozen Court. Everything that…everything that I did to you." Shane stops his wandering hands, moving them to cup Drake's face instead. "I'm sorry, baby. I broke every rule we had. It's only coming back to me now, but, shit, I—"

"Shh. It's okay."

"No!"

"So you made a deal. So you were the stupidest idiot I've ever met." Drake gives him a quick kiss, tasting salt again. "Nothing I didn't already know."

"But I outed you to your Church. I said—god, the most horrible things. I killed people, and things, and I slept with—"

"Shane. Stop. I've had nine years to come to terms with that stuff. It wasn't you, anyway."

Shane sniffs, holding back a nervous laugh. "You got older. I saw, in the Court."

"Yeah, well, not all of us were frozen in time. You think you'll snap back to how you're supposed to be? Get a few matching wrinkles like mine?"

His eyes have adjusted to the darkness just enough to see the appalled look on Shane's face, and just laughs and pulls him close. "You're gonna make it up to me for the next nine years, okay? Sound fair?"

"Next twenty. Next fifty."

"Masochist."

Shane manages a watery chuckle at that. "Some things never change. You were the only thing I never stopped wanting."

Just like that, something inside Drake breaks. He feels his own chest heaving, the choked little sobs becoming real ones, and somehow it winds up with him sitting, Shane kneeling behind him, holding, warm and solid and so, so real.

"Knew it wasn't you," he mutters, and he hates the sound of his own voice when he's crying. He didn't cry when he woke up and Shane wasn't Shane anymore. He didn't cry all the times an empty shell that just looked like his boyfriend showed up drunk and angry on his doorstep, using every bad thing Drake had ever thought about himself against him.

God, he hasn't cried since he was sixteen.

"You—I mean, it's just that it *wasn't* you. Not the guy I've been dealing with for the last fucking decade."

"Careful," Shane warns, and Drake can see some of the humor in his face now that his eyes are adjusting. "You're all churchy now. Can't go around swearing like that, they'll think I'm a bad influence on you."

"I knew," Drake repeats, insistent to the point of ignoring the other man. "No matter what you—*he* said, I knew it wasn't you."

Shane's mouth is on his neck again, wet and hot and sloppy, teeth grazing over a birthmark, hands sliding down over Drake's chest. "Well, baby, who the hell did you think it was? Just because it wasn't my *good* self doesn't mean it was somebody else possessing me."

"But you'd never do that."

"Do what?"

It's harder to think with Shane unbuttoning his shirt, deliberately running his thumb down his sternum. "Like—" He tries to gather his thoughts, tries to be coherent while wanting nothing in the world more than for Shane to continue doing exactly what he's doing. The real Shane touches him differently, waits to see his responses after doing something, takes obvious pleasure in the sheer closeness of their bodies, nuzzling into his neck. It's difficult to think about the bad things, the bad times when it feels like they're over. "You'd never...show up at my apartment and threaten to kill the next person that comes out of their apartment if I didn't let you blow me."

Shane's hand falters, his breath drawing in quick, startled. "I did that?"

"You'd never come to the place where I work and tell everyone I was a child molester."

"I didn't! I—that's a joke, right? You're just saying that, right? I think I'd remember."

"Does that sound like the kind of thing I'd think was funny?" Drake asks quietly, not turning around. "You were angry at me because I told you you weren't welcome at church. That was after you outed me to them. It took me years to get a good amount of students back, and that was after being questioned by the police and going through every background check known to man."

He has more, nine years' worth of Shane drunk, angry, bitter and cruel and far, far too good at humiliating and ruining him, but Shane's trembling against his back, and hot tears are splashing onto his shoulder. "I…" There's a ragged sadness to Shane's voice that he's never heard before. "I…you can't possibly….after all that, you can't possibly want me back. You have to hate me."

"Wasn't you." Drake turns, staying seated, so he can pull Shane up into his lap. "Wasn't you. Like I said."

"But—"

"Wasn't. You." Drake is as firm as he can kindly be, reinforcing his words with gentle touches. "Would you ever do that stuff?"

"No! Of course—"

"Then obviously it wasn't you. Are you sore? Did they…did they rape you?"

Shane shrugs, looking uncomfortable. "Wasn't me, right?"

"But your body—"

Shane bites his neck, sharper than usual, enough to make him jump. "Leave it. Don't you dare treat me like I'm made of broken glass."

"I heard you shatter. I saw the ice go flying. What the hell happened? I thought…I thought you were dead. All of you, not just the way you sort of were for years."

Shane's hands twist in his shirt, not trying to strip it off now, just fisting in it as if it's a security blanket. For that matter, he tucks himself under Drake's arm, for all that they're nearly the same height and he's no lightweight himself. They make it work. They always have, though cuddling's always been an awkward affair that takes some doing. "I don't remember much of those last few moments. I was…I was so angry at him. And then I wasn't feeling much of anything, and that was what made him angry. I think he wanted me to suffer more. So he gave my soul back right as I turned to ice, so I'd be trapped like that forever."

"But…you weren't." Drake can't help himself, and he runs his hands all over Shane's body, making absolutely sure that there's no hidden pocket of ice, no lurking nasty secret. Shane's as warm as ever, oddly hot to the touch, the same way he's been as long as Drake can remember. "You got out. I didn't think anyone could do that."

Shane shifts in his lap, sensuous and immediate, grinding his ass down between Drake's legs. "Yeah, well, I do a lot of crazy things. You still love me, right?"

Drake grabs his hips, intending to hold him still, to keep him focused. It's not as easy as it sounds when Shane's arching like that, that gorgeous ass rubbing slowly up and down. "S-stop it. Of course I love you. As long as you don't make any more stupid deals."

"I promise."

"And you start trying to wash the dishes right after they get dirty."

"Sure, sure."

"And you don't vanish to leave me in charge of your plants for nine years."

He doesn't need to see Shane's face to know he's grinning. "Don't tell me you kept them alive for all that time."

"Of course I did! I told you I'd look after them if you died, and—"

"They really don't live that long, baby. You replaced them with other ones, didn't you?"

Drake buries his head between Shane's shoulder blades, tracing the lines of lean muscle with his nose, his lips. "I just thought…if you did ever figure out a way to come back to me, I knew you'd want your plants. That's all."

"You never gave up on me, huh?"

"Never."

"You're an idiot."

He's deflecting and changing the subject so he doesn't have to explain how he got out of the ice. Or what the Ice King meant when he called him "Child of Flame." "That's me," Drake says wearily, letting go of Shane's hips and letting him wriggle all he wants. "I'm just a big idiot."

"My idiot?"

That almost sends Drake over the edge again. Not because he's Shane's, of *course*, but because he's playful when he's needy, shy about actually wanting something of value, like a promise, when he's always been thoroughly convinced he's not worth anything of the sort, even from Drake. Maybe especially from Drake.

"Yeah. Your idiot."

Just like you're mine.

And damned if anyone's ever going to Shane from him again.

Chapter Eleven

Shane thinks he's doing a damn good job of holding it together.

It's not easy when every bit of him wants to tremble, to just break down and collapse on the floor and let Drake pick him up, let Drake carry him home and put him to bed and curl up with him for the foreseeable future. At the same time, he wants to scream, to laugh, to just run around the city naked and feel beautifully, gloriously *alive* for the first time in years, and no matter how little he remembers, he can't have properly appreciated the smell of the city, the bracing fresh wind, the feel of the snow between his toes, the—

Okay, he's freezing.

"Where's your car?" he mumbles into Drake's arm, muffled against the smooth cotton of his torn shirt.

"The Soul-Thief tore it up pretty bad. We've been taking yours."

Shane's fairly certain that he doesn't own a car, but that's hardly going to help him now. Besides, the less he can remind Drake of what a soulless bastard he's been for the last several years, the better. He's got more than enough to make up for already without adding anything.

"Here. You must be freezing."

"Drake, what the—you can't give me your shirt, we'll look like a pair of goddamn refugees, what are—"

"You can't just go around naked! Better refugees than arrested!"

It doesn't take them long to get back to Drake's place, not even on foot. Then again, it's possible Shane just doesn't notice the distance because he's so unfathomably glad to be back.

Drake opens the door to his apartment, scratching at his hair the way he does when he's nervous. It's a familiar habit, something Shane's pretty sure he's missed. "Sorry about the mess. I haven't really had much time lately for cleaning and stuff."

It's a pretty exceptional mess. Shane's lost count of the times he's teased Drake about it, but right now it doesn't seem important. It's not gross, just piles of papers and clothes and books everywhere, and Shane grins. "It looks like the rare librarian-bird tried to make a nest in here."

"Very funny."

"Is there still a bed?"

"You're showering before you get in it. We both are. A lot of people exploded in that hall."

"I was shielding us," Shane points out, but he's far from being angry, not when he's in a place that is so clearly *Drake's* place. Nothing ever makes him feel more at home than being surrounded by Drake.

The shower is tiny, far too small for two people. That turns out to be a blessing a few minutes later, when Shane breaks down sobbing under the hot water, eventually throwing up a magical sound shield to keep Drake from hearing.

Pathetic.

Drake is a good man, one of the best in the world, but surely he has his limits. Sure, it seems like everything's going to be good again, but it can't be that easy. Nothing ever is, not for him. Not for them. It's not possible that after so much stress, so much separation, so much *hurt* everything could just snap back to normal.

And it's all his fault.

Shane's pretty far out of it by the time Drake comes in, switching off the shower and lifting him easily into his arms. He doesn't say anything, just towels him dry before getting him into the bedroom, which is thankfully a lot less cluttered than the rest of the apartment.

"G-god," Shane chokes out, shivering and clutching, "I'm a f-f-fucking mess."

Drake chuckles. "You have no idea how much I prefer you like this. God, I've missed you."

Shane gives up on dignity for the evening, clinging to his boyfriend with arms and legs, nestling into his neck. "What now?"

"Now?"

"Yeah. I'm not exactly gonna be raking in a paycheck as First Vassal anymore. How attached are you to being Champion?"

"Why do you ask? I don't mind supporting us on what I make from the studio. I mean, this isn't exactly a big place, but—"

"You don't want to go back to hunting? I thought you quit because you didn't have a partner anymore, but I'll do whatever you want."

Drake's hands are broad and rough down his back, stroking up and down his spine. It's good, more of a gentle ease back into life than anything Shane's felt in years, and he arches back into it. "I don't know. There's a lot of powerful stuff out there. What if we meet something else we can't handle? What if I get hurt again? I...I want to be able to trust you not to do anything stupid, but—"

"I *won't*. You can trust me. God, do you think there's anyone who hasn't learned their lesson more than me?" That starts to bring on the shakes again, so he stops, blinking back more tears. He distracts himself by looking around the room, hunting for any little clues about Drake's life he's missed or just can't remember. "You like teaching kids?"

"Kind of. I like seeing them get better. I like teaching women's self-defense. Makes me feel like I'm doing some good."

"You're a Champion of the Church."

"Are you implying I don't need to do anything else good because my ass is karmically covered?"

"No, I'm saying you'll have to teach a hell of a lot of women how to fight off rapists before you can balance out the damage the Church has done."

"You're a dick."

"You never prayed. Not once that I can remember, and I lived with you for ten years. Then all of a sudden, what, I'm gone and you find God?" That's what's bothering him, Shane realizes. No matter what Drake's title might be, there's not a single religious item anywhere in the room.

Drake is quiet for a second, in the way that means he's thinking rather than angry, and Shane gives him time to put his thoughts together. Just because he's not quick-witted all of the time doesn't make him stupid, and Shane's seen too many people find that out the hard way. "I asked them, when they signed me up. I asked if it was okay that I stopped believing years ago."

"And?"

"And…they said something interesting. They were glad. Because people who take this job see things all the time that make them question their faith. They see people so powerful they could easily fake miracles, and things so evil it's impossible to imagine that God lets them continue to exist on earth. They get freaked out, and they have existential crises or breakdowns and wind up hesitating at a crucial moment the first time someone claims to be the next coming of Christ."

Vaguely, Shane thinks he remembers something about a trick he and a couple other Vassals had played on the Church's prior Champion, back long ago at the beginning of his tenure under the Ice King. Though the memories are hazy, he can sort of remember *someone* claiming to be Jesus, and he definitely remembers that it was hilarious.

Oops.

"So they prefer atheists?"

"Not exactly. They said…they said it didn't matter whether I believed or not, as long as I lived every day exactly as I would if

I were certain there *was* a God."

Drake looks all set to explain himself further, but Shane nods. "Makes sense. Cool. So, you want to stay on there?"

"I do good work. I protect people from evil."

"You sap." Shane wriggles in his arms, turning to mouth wet kisses down Drake's neck, his chest, down to his stomach. "Knight in shining denim, huh?"

"Would you prefer I take them off?"

"Yep." Crying fit over, Shane's fingers run along the waistband of those worn denim jeans, his lips ghosting over the muscles of Drake's abdomen. "You got fat."

"Did not!"

"Cute fat. You used to have a six-pack."

"I still—"

"Oh, it's still there, but now you're all soft and squishy on top of it." Shane pinches his stomach, then gasps as Drake grabs his hair. "Oh, sensitive, are we?"

"Not all of us had an unnatural deal with the devil to keep us young and perfect," Drake grumbles, glaring down at him. "Metabolism's a bitch after thirty."

"God, you're so old." Shane drags down his zipper, nimbly unfastening the button and stripping off every bit of clothing. "You sure you can still keep up with me? Like you said, I didn't get old and fat."

"Call me fat again," Drake warns, a hint of challenge in his voice that gets Shane harder than almost anything.

"Why, you horny to smack me around? You miss that, baby?" Shane tosses the towel onto the floor with Drake's jeans, moving up to straddle his, slowly rubbing his hardening cock against Drake's stomach. "Because I sure as hell did."

It's difficult for Shane to qualify why he finds that guilt, that hesitation, that shame on Drake's face to be so fucking cute. "You don't have to treat me like I'm fragile," he reminds the other man, grinding slowly downward, feeling Drake's thick cock get harder under his ass. "F-fuck, I'm not that delicate, no one else treats me like I'm breakable."

"I'm not anyone else." There's something intense and worried in Drake's eyes, enough that it almost makes Shane stop rubbing his ass down against him.

Well, almost.

"I'm in love with you. That's supposed to mean I take care of you."

"You *do*. Stop being an idiot and *fuck* me, it's been goddamn years."

It hasn't, not really. He sort of remembers that he's had Drake several times in the last nine years, though not on any sort of regular schedule. He's pretty sure Drake tried to make it work when he first lost his soul, and even after he left had consented to the occasional drunken fuck against the wall. Hell, he's fairly certain that he's been fucked by Drake a few times just in the last couple days.

"You should have a bruise here," Drake murmurs, stroking over his hip. "I gave it to you in the alley."

"Sorry. Healed it in the shower. I wasn't sure what was from who and I didn't want anyone else's marks on me."

He realizes the second after the words leave his mouth what a mistake that is to say. "Um…I mean…"

"You can heal bruises?" Drake demands, hands suddenly tight around his waist, sitting up. "All this time, you've been able to heal bruises, cuts, little shit like that? You said you could only do the big stuff!"

Shane chews on his bottom lip, wriggling guiltily against Drake's hands. Not how he planned to get him riled up, but it's working. "Well, I like having them from you. I was afraid you'd make me get rid of them if you knew I could."

He's on his back in a second, then flipped around to his hands and knees. "Maybe I should give you a whole new set, huh?"

Shane wiggles his ass, grinning down at the pillows. "Yes please."

Drake isn't gentle. He rarely is, especially when he's really horny, really angry, and Shane loves it. He knows how difficult it is to get Drake to lose control, and revels in being the one that it's *easy* for. Every smack of Drake's hand gets him harder, every forming bruise only making him writhe back, panting, "Fuck me, fuck me, please, baby, fuck me."

"Whore. You get off on me hurting you."

"What was your first fucking clue, Sherlock?"

He cries out at the next slap to his ass, a little too low, reddening his upper thigh in what's probably going to be a pretty impressive hand-print.

"I think you should stop talking so dirty and get your mouth down on my cock," Drake breathes in his ear, and Shane shakes his head.

"Can't. Please, just fuck me, I'll suck you off after, I need it, please."

Drake nips at his earlobe, dragging big fingers up to spread his ass apart. "You worried you're gonna come while you're sucking me off?"

Shane nods, not bothering to deny it.

He has no idea when Drake managed to grab the lube, or even where he keeps it these days. All he manages is to be relieved when a couple slick fingers trace over his hole, then push inside.

Shane lets out a long, keening moan, collapsing forward to bury his face onto his forearms. "F-fuck."

"Can you take more?"

"Fuck *yes* I can take more, give me your fucking cock!"

Drake's hand cracks down hard over his ass again, and all of Shane's breath leaves him in a yelp. "Quiet. The walls here are thinner than our old place."

"Then we're fucking moving tomorrow!"

Drake slides in a third finger, and Shane's thighs start trembling. Just because he's taken more doesn't mean it isn't thick, doesn't fill him with that delicious spreading ache that runs up his spine and makes him pant, makes him whine.

"You gonna come?"

Shane nods, no breath left to do anything else, his cock painfully hard and dripping onto the sheets.

Drake pulls out his fingers, and Shane swears violently, creatively, in three or four languages. "Fuck you! Put them back in or I'll fucking kill you!"

Drake flips him over again onto his back and backhands him across the face. The pain is sharp and immediate, and does less than nothing to ease his erection. Drake had joked once that he could make Shane come just by slapping him around long enough, though every attempt to prove or disprove his words has always ended with them forgetting the point and fucking past the point of exhaustion.

It doesn't look like tonight will be any different.

Drake slides up until the head of his cock rubs against Shane's lips, only laughing when Shane tries to lick it, straining up against the weight of Drake straddling his chest. "Hungry for my cock? You sure look like you want to get it in your mouth."

"Please." Shane hears his own voice come out low and husky, pleading, whorish. He tries again, lips parted and eager, and Drake holds his head down.

He leans forward, smearing his lips with clear fluid, tongue flicking out to taste, and this time Drake doesn't tease him. He slides in, slow, relentless, letting every thick inch of his cock fill Shane's mouth. "You're so good at taking me," he says softly, reaching down to stroke Shane's hair even as he holds him in place. "I missed your mouth so much." Shane's hips twitch upward, rutting against empty air and wishing it was something, because he's so hard he hurts, and with the way Drake's sitting on him he can't even reach down for his own cock. The tears in his eyes are more from frustration and need than from pain or gagging as Drake stuffs his mouth full, dragging hot and bitter across his tongue, and the taste alone almost makes Shane come without being touched.

"You're cute when you're desperate. You can breathe?"

Shane glares cross-eyed at him, the very epitome of *if I couldn't, you'd fucking know about it.*

Not knowing one's strength is all very well. Drake's a huge guy, but he knows his own strength plenty. It's Shane's strength he always seems to forget about. Then again, if he really *had* forgotten, he wouldn't be sitting on Shane's chest and stuffing his cock down the other man's throat.

Shane twists and writhes under him, slurping hungrily at the thick hard flesh in his mouth, only too aware of how slutty, how desperate he sounds, and god, if only his hands were free, it would only take a single pull of his dick to make him come.

"You're perfect," Drake grunts, riding his face hard, forcing every last inch down his throat, holding him close, fucking his face hard without pulling out more than a couple inches. He holds his hair, holds his head, arms pinioned with his legs, the solid bulk of him a reassuring weight. "I bet you could come just from having my cock down your throat, huh? You don't care where you get it as long as you get fucked."

It's close to true, and Shane's certainly far beyond words, beyond anything but pathetic humping up into the air, dragging his tongue frantically down Drake's cock, determined to make it good for him, show him how much better he is than that horrible pale imitation he's been dealing with. Irony or not, he's made up his mind to outdo himself, and show that old version of himself how superior he is.

More than anything, he just wants Drake to come in his mouth.

The look on Drake's face changes, something pleading, needing, as wanting as it is controlling. "You hungry, baby? You want me to come in your mouth? You gonna swallow it all?"

It's nearly impossible to talk, to even nod around the thick cock filling his mouth, but oh, Shane tries. He tries with every twitch, every thrash of his willing body, every blink of his watering eyes.

Drake strokes his face with one thumb, wiping the tears away. "Good boy." He pulls out, breathing hard, and works his hand over his cock, the other still supporting Shane's head. "Open your mouth. Wide."

Shane does as he's told, licking his lips, tasting Drake on them already. "Please," he whispers, eyes locked on Drake's hand, pumping himself fast. "Please, I need it, please."

"I said open," Drake growls, and Shane obeys just as Drake comes, filling his mouth, some spilling out to drip down his lips and chin.

At a nod from Drake, he swallows, tongue flicking out to lick up the drops he's missed, then collapses back onto the bed with a sigh. "Please, baby," he begs softly, "you're going to kill me."

"What do you want?" Drake slides off him, pressing a kiss to his cheek.

"I..." Shane swallows again, hands fisting in the sheets to keep from just grabbing his own cock and yanking until he's done. "God, baby, I want everything. I want you to fuck me and I want to fuck you and I want to fuck your mouth and I want to ride your hand until I come all over your face and—I need to come, baby, I'm not making much sense."

"You're making plenty of sense to me." A little flush creeps over Drake's cheeks, and he nods. "You want to fuck me?"

A low shudder rakes through Shane's body. As hazy as his memory is, he knows damned well that he hasn't had Drake's ass in a decade. A little grin plays over his lips as he squeezes the base of his cock, trying to regain some measure of control over himself. "You know, I got fucked plenty. But I'm willing to bed that you haven't had anything in your ass since I sold my soul."

"Good thing I'm not a betting man, huh?"

Shane groans, lurching forward and flipping Drake onto his hands and knees, getting a knee up between Drake's legs to spread them wide. He leans over, breath hot as he murmurs into Drake's ear, "I know you like being on your back, but trust me, this'll be easier. You can always look at my pretty face later."

He kisses his way down Drake's back, tasting the remnants of soap from the shower, of sweat from the last hour or so, of *Drake* the same as ever. "Mm...wider, baby. Spread your legs for me."

"Shane, no, I told you, I don't like—"

Shane laughs, squeezing Drake's ass, urging his cheeks apart. "Nah. I heard you fucking wailing last time I did this."

"That's—that doesn't prove—"

"Tell me honestly you don't like it, and I won't. Or is this just one of those little things you do, like when you let me top at first because you were afraid your cock was too big for me?"

Drake buries his head in the pillows, muttering something that sounds an awful lot like, "Didn't know what a goddamn size queen you were."

"Are," Shane corrects him cheerfully, and swipes his tongue over Drake's hole.

He relishes the way it makes the big man buck and moan, drawing different sounds than he ever hears normally. He delves his tongue inside, and there's a sense of power, of exhilaration in seeing someone as powerful as Drake come totally, completely undone.

He wonders if this is what Drake sees, when it's the other way around. He's wondered before, never quite daring to ask.

It's not a fabulous time for introspection, not when he has Drake totally at his mercy with every swipe and lick of his tongue. It's good, but he pulls away after a few minutes and sure enough Drake thrusts back eagerly, a needy slew of noises falling from his mouth as he begs, "More...more, please, I swear I won't complain about it again."

"You sure you don't want me to fuck you?"

Drake rearranges himself in an instant, knees braced wide apart on the bed, head bowed in what looks like surrender. "I—no. Fuck me, please. I...I really want you inside me."

Shane presses a kiss to his shoulder blade, smiling as he

murmurs, "I love you, baby."

He's gentle with Drake, no matter how Drake is when the positions are reversed. It's not about revenge, never is, and all the revenge Shane could ever want is to see Drake thrashing and writhing because of something Shane does, because of the way Shane touches him, Shane fucks him.

Then again, given how eagerly Drake thrusts back onto his fingers, maybe he's overestimating the other man's need for gentleness. "You don't feel as rusty as I'd expect," Shane pants, withdrawing his fingers and slicking up his cock, making sure he's dripping with lube. It's never as easy this way, but god, the faces, the sounds Drake makes are always worth it. He can feel a tremble raking through Drake's body, like he's caught an anxious rabbit instead of a burly Champion of God.

"I, uh, don't think you're supposed to find any rust in there, really."

"Jesus, Drake, leave the wisecracks to me. You haven't been fucking around, have you?"

Drake shoots him a look, copper fire burning in his eyes as he twists around. "Say that again," he challenges, and Shane backs off.

Secretly, the reaction pleases him, more than he wants to admit. It's selfish and horrible, but Drake is his, has been forever. "No, it's good. Just means you've really got to be aching for my cock by now."

Drake's hand comes up over his shoulder, and Shane twines their fingers together, feeling Drake's heartbeat pulse under his skin. "Just go slow, okay? It's been a while since I even did anything with my fingers."

Mentally, Shane nearly loses it at that image, of Drake in his lonely shitty little bed, thrusting down onto his fingers like they're Shane's cock, thinking of no one but him. Out loud, he just says, "Of course."

The second the head of his cock breaches that tight ring of muscle, he bites his lip, hoping he'll be able to keep that promise.

It's shockingly tight, almost painful, and it doesn't help his resolve to go slow that Drake is shoving back onto him like he's hungry for more.

Shane gives him a breathless little laugh, fingers digging deep into Drake's hips, surrounded by the sight of him, the smell of him, the taste of his skin, and mutters, "Go easy on me, baby, I'm trying to be a gentleman here."

Drake clenches even harder at that, and Shane sees stars. Involuntarily, he thrusts in harder than he means to, and that feels so good he nearly loses his mind.

Everything is chaos after that, Drake grunting and slamming back onto him, Shane thrusting deep into that tight heat with every snap of his hips, arms curled possessively around Drake's chest and torso, one hand stealing down to curl around Drake's cock.

He can see Drake fisting a hand in the sheets, hear his frantic, pleading breaths as he rocks back, mouth falling open at the sensation of being filled. For a minute, Shane's jealous, but he squashes that feeling easily enough. It feels good enough to be buried to the hilt in Drake's ass that he doesn't mind topping every once in a while. And better than that is the expression on Drake's face, urgent, overwhelmed, shivering at how full of cock he is and still grinding back for more.

"Inside," Drake breathes, voice hoarse, muscles tense under his skin as he rocks, his own cock hard again and dripping onto Shane's hand. "Need you to."

In that second, Shane regrets nothing.

He doesn't regret selling his soul, no matter what horrible things followed, no matter what happened. If he hadn't, Drake would be dead, and probably Shane too, and none of this would ever have come to pass.

He'd said before that he'd do anything for Drake, anything for his love, anything to keep him. He'd never said they would all be good things.

Drake cries out as he comes, spilling over Shane's hand, and the rippling squeeze around Shane's cock is too much, far too much for him to handle, as aroused as he is. He bites into Drake's shoulder, not quite hard enough to break the skin, just enough to muffle all the embarrassing things he might accidentally say as he loses all control, clinging to Drake as if they're the last people on Earth. It's too intense, robbing him of breath, of sight, of any concept of time and his own body. A shattering, burning thing that overwhelms him totally, narrowing everything he knows to the sensation of being buried inside the man he loves.

He can feel his heartbeat pulsing loud beneath his skin, the only sound besides their breathing in the still night air. He can't move, as much as his muscles twitch and jump, every part of him completely overwhelmed as the sweat cools on his back.

Usually, Drake likes him to pull out right away, not overly fond of the sensation of having anything inside of him when he's not aroused, not feeling that needing ache. Now, when Shane moves to pull out, Drake puts a hand on his wrist. "Not yet. When you have to."

Shane presses a gentle, tired kiss to the back of his shoulder.

Outside the window, the building next to Drake's erupts into flames.

Shane almost wants to laugh. He lowers his forehead to Drake's back with a groan, muttering, "I think I have to."

"Yeah. Let me grab the sword."